A Soldier'<

Maude Mary Butler

Alpha Editions

This edition published in 2023

ISBN : 9789357961707

Design and Setting By
Alpha Editions
www.alphaedis.com
Email - info@alphaedis.com

Contents

CHAPTER 1.--HOME FROM THE WAR.

The war was over--the cruel, cruel war; and Father and Uncle Howard were on their way home. Children's voices, in every key of joy and thanksgiving, sang the happy news from morning to night. The white, strained look faded from Mother's face, and she became her old, bright self again.

Now that they were over, the children tried to forget how long and sad and weary the days had been during which the sight of the post-bag, and the morning newspaper, almost took everyone's breath away, until the columns of "War news" had been hastily scanned before taking letters and papers to Mother's room.

Then came the day when Uncle Howard's name was amongst the "seriously wounded," and there was a brief account of how he had saved the guns, and then returning into the firing line to pick up a wounded soldier, had himself been dangerously wounded.

The children thought of Uncle Howard's delicate young motherless boy, and sobbed: "Poor, poor Carol."

They did not know how to break the news to Mother, because Uncle Howard was her twin brother, and they all knew how dearly she loved him. Unperceived she had entered the room, and had learned the news for herself. The days that followed were darker than before, for it was not known for some weeks if Major Willmar would live or die. Gradually, slightly better news came, and he was pronounced out of danger. Later on it was announced he was ordered home, and Father, Colonel Mandeville, was coming with him.

As soon as the vessel left Cape Town the children began their happy, joyous preparations for the welcome home. Then, in the midst of them, when the triumphal arches were erected, awaiting only the final floral decorations, came a telegram from Gibraltar. Major Willmar had suffered a relapse at sea, and the doctors had not been able to save him. His body had been committed to the waves.

Again the children sobbed: "Poor, poor Carol."

Mother was strangely calm and quiet. "Carol must come to us. We must take the place to him of all he has lost," she said.

She wrote to the lady who had charge of him, asking her to take the boy to meet the vessel at Plymouth, in order that Colonel Mandeville might bring Carol home with him.

All the children, seven in number, were at the station when the express drew up. Edith and Gwendolin, two tall fair girls of twelve and thirteen years; Percy and Frank, eleven and ten; then three of the dearest little maidens, Sylvia four, Estelle three, and the sweet Rosebud, whom Father had never seen. She had come to cheer Mother's breaking heart in the dark days of the war, and was now two years old.

It was an unusual occurrence for an express train to stop at that quiet country station. The porters were on the alert to drag out the luggage as quickly as possible. A tall bronzed and bearded man sprang out of the train on the instant of stopping, so changed that even the elder children scarcely recognized him.

He looked at them with hungry eyes, as if he would take them all in his arms at once, had they been big enough to go round, then seized the smallest of all, the little snow-white maiden.

"Iz 'ou Daddy?" she asked.

"I am Daddy, my little white Rosebud." One by one he took each in his strong arms. All looking to him, no one noticed the boy who had followed him out of the railway carriage, who was now looking on with wondering eyes. Rosebud was the first to speak to him. "Iz 'ou Tarol?" she asked. Stooping, he too folded his arms around her, not such strong arms as her father's, but very loving. From that moment the little maiden became one of the dearest things in life to the boy.

"Where's Mother, children?"

"Mother did not feel quite able to come to the station, Father. She bore the news of dear Uncle's death so well at first; then she broke down entirely, and she has not left her room since," Edith told him. The Colonel then remembered the boy who had accompanied him.

"Children, here is Carol."

They quickly gave him the loving welcome which their sympathetic hearts prompted. Father suggested sending on the carriage, saying to the children:

"We will walk through the park. Oh, the sweet breath of the dear home land, after Africa's sultry heat!"

Carol kept hold of Rosebud's hand. The little maiden was a revelation to him, never having had little sisters or brothers of his own. His mother for a long time before her death had been a hopeless invalid, and whilst she was slowly dying of consumption the boy had developed tubercular disease of the left hip, and the physicians, who pronounced it a hopeless case, also said one lung was affected. Three years the boy lay on his back on a couch, or in a spinal carriage, and it was generally anticipated he would quickly follow his mother to an early grave. But after Mrs. Willmar's death a cousin of hers came from America to take charge of the motherless boy, and from the day that she came he began to get better. Now, as he walked with his cousins across the park, though somewhat tall for his twelve years and extremely slight of stature, he bore no trace of his past sufferings.

On arriving at the Manor, Colonel Mandeville went straight to his wife's room, mounting the staircase two steps at a time. The children took Carol to the school-room, saying, "Mother will send for you presently, dear Carol."

School-room tea was ready, and to their great delight the three little girls, who belonged of course to the nursery, were invited to be present. Before they sat down each child had a little offering to make Carol, not a new gift they had bought for him, but one of their own treasures, just to make him feel how glad they were to have him: that henceforth he was to be their own dear brother.

It was all so strange and new to him, he did not know how to thank them. Rosebud's offering of her little white bunny was so perfectly sweet. It became a treasure of treasures to him ever after. He was strangely quiet, but there seemed no sadness in his eyes or voice. His cousins could not understand it, and even wondered if he had loved his father as they loved theirs.

Tea was just finished when the message came for Carol to go to Mother's room. All the children wanted to accompany him, but the maid who brought the message said: "Only Master Carol was to go," and she led the boy to Mrs. Mandeville's room.

Carol had only once before seen his aunt. She had visited his home in Devonshire when his mother was very ill, and he himself had been too ill to care or notice who came and went.

Mrs. Mandeville was lying on a couch in her boudoir. She was a tall, fair woman, of a gentle yielding nature, and a beautiful countenance. Never strong or robust, for some years she had been subject to attacks of nervous prostration. The joyous excitement of her husband's safe return, and the grief for her brother's death, had brought on one of these attacks. She sobbed aloud as she drew Carol into her arms and held him closely to her.

"My darling boy!"

"Auntie, dear, do not grieve like this."

"Carol, I loved your father very, very, dearly."

"But, Auntie, that should make you not grieve for him. Cousin Alicia has taught me to feel so glad and happy about Father. I could not cry or be sorry now. I love to think how he gave his life for that poor, wounded soldier. Jesus said there was no greater love than to lay down one's life for a friend, and it was not even a friend; it was a stranger. Some day there will be no more war, because everyone will know that God is our Father, and His name is Love. But we are only His children as we reflect Him--reflect Love. When everyone understands this, no one will want war."

Mrs. Mandeville looked with surprise at the earnest young face, so calmly confident of what he said.

"It is nice to see you, Carol, looking so well and strong. You were very ill when I saw you two years ago. We have never been able to understand your recovery. What a mistake the doctors must have made about your case."

"Auntie, they did not make a mistake. It was Cousin Alicia who taught me about Christian Science. Then I began to get well, and I soon lost the dreadful pain in my hip."

"Carol, dear, never mention a word about Christian Science before your Uncle Raymond. He says it is dreadful heresy, and it makes him so angry to hear it talked about. Did he meet you at the station?"

"No, Auntie. I have not seen him yet."

"He said he would meet the train but he generally manages to get too late. He will be here this evening for dinner."

Uncle Raymond was Mrs. Mandeville's brother, and the rector of the parish.

"But, Auntie, if he asks anything about my illness I must tell him what has made me well."

"I do not think he will, dear; so there will be no need to say anything. It is very beautiful, Carol, for you to think Christian Science has healed you, and there is no need for your faith to be shaken."

"I do not *think*, Auntie, I *know*, so that no one could shake my faith."

"Well, dear, we won't talk about it. Tell me, did you have a pleasant journey?"

"Yes, Auntie, a very pleasant journey; Uncle was so kind to me."

"I am sure he would be, Carol. You are glad to come to us, darling--to be our own dear son? You will feel this is home, and your cousins not cousins, but brothers and sisters?"

"Yes, Auntie. I know my father wished me to come to you--but--I am sorry to leave Cousin Alicia. I love her so much."

"Of course, darling, that is only natural. She has been quite a mother to you since your own dear mother died."

Carol did not speak; a choking sensation of pain prevented him. He knew that Cousin Alicia had been more than a mother to him.

"May I write to her to-night, Auntie? She will like to hear from me."

"Of course, dear. Write to her as often as you like."

"I think that will be every day then," the boy said promptly, with a smile. Mrs. Mandeville smiled too.

"Dear boy, how you have comforted me. I feel so much better for this little talk with you. Perhaps I shall be able to surprise everybody, and go down to dinner this evening."

"Oh, Auntie, please do. At tea Edith said, 'It would be just lovely if only Mother could come down to dinner.' We can nearly always do what we want to do, Auntie."

"Can we, dear? Then go and write your letter now, and do not mention to anyone that I am going to try to surprise them this evening."

CHAPTER II.--CAROL'S LETTER.

"MANOR HOUSE

MANDEVILLE.

"*Dear Cousin Alicia,*

"It seemed such a long journey before we arrived here. Uncle was so kind and told me about the different places as we passed through. But I felt I was getting such a long way from you, as we passed town after town. All my cousins were at the station to meet us; but Auntie was not well enough to be there. I should like to describe them all to you, but I am sure I could not. They are ever so much nicer than any of the children I have read about in books. I will only tell you their names. Perhaps you will see them all some day. Edith, Gwendolin, Percy, and Frank, in the school-room; and in the nursery, Sylvia, Estelle, and Rosebud. Uncle had never seen Rosebud. She is two years and three months old, and is the sweetest little girl. She has such pretty ways. I do love to hear her talk.

"We walked from the station through the park. Uncle seemed so glad to see his own home again. The Manor House is very old; such quaint little oriel windows, and turrets, and gables. I have not learned my way about yet, but the school-room and nurseries are quite close together. It was returning from Auntie's boudoir to the schoolroom I got lost, and I found myself in quite a different part of the house. I opened a door I thought was the school-room, and it was the housekeeper's room. Then a maid took me to the school-room. Percy and Frank thought it very amusing, and said they could find their way anywhere blindfold, and Rosebud said 'Me tome wiff 'ou, Tarol.' I didn't see Auntie until after tea. We all had tea together in the school-room, the nursery children as well. The governess invited them. Her name is Miss Markham, she is very strict, but I think she is kind too. I am thinking all the time of the history of England when she speaks, and wondering what part of it she belongs to. The elder children are going down to dinner, as it is Uncle's first evening at home.

"Auntie was lying on a couch when I was taken to her room. She seemed so full of grief and sadness. She wept when she held her arms around me. But I just knew that Love is everywhere, and sorrow and sadness cannot be where Love is. In a little while she was quite different, and even smiled as she talked to me. She said I had comforted her so. I would have liked to explain to her what had comforted her, but she does not like me to say anything about Christian Science, and asked me not to mention it before Uncle Raymond, because it makes him angry. Auntie thinks I could not have been so ill as the doctors thought, or I should not be quite well and strong now. Please tell me, dear Cousin, will it be denying Christ, if I do not tell people what healed me? I did so wish I could have told Auntie some of the beautiful things you have taught me. Will you write to me very often, please? I am going to write nearly every day to you. Auntie says I may--as often as I like. I have such a dear little room all to myself, so I shall be able to do the Lesson-Sermon every morning before breakfast. Thank you again for giving me *Science and Health* for my very own, and the Bible which was my mother's. I want to study both books so well that when I am a man I shall know them better than anything else in the world. I am to study with Edith and Gwendolin for the present. Frank and Percy go to a large public school at H--. I am to go with them when Uncle is quite sure I am strong enough. He does not understand that I am perfectly well and strong. I must leave off now. I have to put on my Eton suit for dinner. I do not feel so far away from you as when I was in the train. It is just as if you were in the room with me. I can feel your thoughts like loving arms around me.

"Dear Cousin Alicia

"Your loving Carol.

"*P.S.* Bed-time. The post-bag had gone when I had finished my letter. I just want to tell you, Auntie came down to dinner. Every one was so surprised and delighted and we had such a happy evening. Uncle played games with us after dinner, and Auntie looked on. The time went so quickly, we were sorry when Uncle said: 'Bed-time, children. To your tents: double quick march.' So we all had to scamper away. Uncle Raymond came to dinner. He is so grave and stern, so different from Father. He went into the study whilst Uncle was playing with us."

CHAPTER III.--A FORBIDDEN BOOK.

Carol had always been a lonely boy. The companionship of other children was a pleasure he had never known. In the remote Devonshire village, where all the years of his young life had been spent, there were no children who could be invited to his home as friends and companions for him. First his mother's delicate health, and then his own, had prevented visits to or from his cousins. When he was seven years old a fall from his pony caused an injury to his hip, which eventually developed into what the doctors diagnosed as tubercular disease of the hip bone. For three years his mother had been slowly dying of consumption, and the boy had been the joy and brightness of her life. She did not live long after she was told that what she was suffering from he would suffer, too, in another form. She died about six months before the war broke out in South Africa, and fulfilling a promise made some time before, a favorite cousin, then resident in America, whose girlhood had been spent with her as a sister, came to take charge of the household and the young motherless invalid. Major Willmar was ordered to the front shortly after operations commenced, but before he went he had hopes that his boy would grow well and strong. There had been such a marked change in him from the day Cousin Alicia arrived, bringing to that saddened home love and--Truth.

It can, therefore, be easily understood that the first few days at the Manor were to Carol days almost of bewilderment. As soon as his cousins found that their joy in having Father back again, safe and sound, did not hurt Carol, nothing restrained their wild exuberance of spirits. They could not understand the gentle, reserved boy, who spoke with so much love and tenderness of his father, yet had no tears or sadness because he would return no more.

"Perhaps he doesn't quite understand," said Gwendolin.

"I think he does," said Edith, "and I am sure he loved Uncle as much as we love Father. There is such a far-away look in his eyes, when he speaks of his father and mother, just as if he were looking at something we cannot see. Although he is so gentle and kind, especially to the little ones, I am sure no one could persuade him to do anything he thought wrong. He is a dear boy. I am glad he is going to study with us for the present, because the boys at school would not understand him. Even Percy and Frank are inclined to mistake his gentleness for weakness. Yet I could imagine him standing and facing any real danger, when most boys would run away."

From the first Edith had conceived a great affection for her Cousin Carol, and, as a consequence, she understood him better. On many occasions she was able to help him, when Percy and Frank were somewhat brusque and impatient in their treatment of him. They could not understand his reluctance to join in some of their games. He loved to look on; but everything was new and strange to him. He had never been used to playing the games which were so much to Frank and Percy. Edith then quietly explained to her less thoughtful brothers that they should not expect a boy who had spent three years on an invalid's couch to be able to play the games in which they were so proficient.

Carol was often in the nursery, Nurse was so big and motherly. She had welcomed him, as if he had been one of her own children from the first. It was a fixed idea amongst the children that as long as there had been a Manor House, Nurse had presided over the nursery. She was always ready to tell them stories of their father and uncles and aunts in the old days. She even had tales of their grandfather, and many past generations of Mandevilles, and in all the stories, of however long ago, they imagined Nurse playing part. One thing they never could imagine: that was the Manor House without her.

When the little girls wanted him, and that was very frequently, Carol was always ready to go to the nursery, and often accompanied them on their walks. Percy and Frank considered it much beneath their dignity to take a walk "with the babies."

The improvement in Mrs. Mandeville's health, which had commenced on Carol's first visit to her room, continued. In a few days she had taken her usual place in the household, and the children rejoiced in the nightly visits to their bedrooms. How glad they were when there were no visitors downstairs, and they could keep her quite a long time.

Upon the occasion of her first visit to Carol's room, she found him sitting up in bed, reading. She had expected to find him asleep, as the other children had detained her so long.

"My little book-worm, what is the story you find so interesting?" she asked playfully, intending to tell him lovingly the next morning that she did not like the children to read in bed.

"Auntie, it isn't a story book. It is _Science and Health_. I read it every night and morning."

"What a very strange book for a little boy to be interested in! The title sounds quite alarmingly dry."

"Oh, Auntie, have you never heard of it? It is such a wonderful book. I am beginning to understand it now. At first I could not, but Cousin Alicia used to explain it so beautifully to me, and now I love to read it."

"I cannot say I remember the title, dear, but I should like to look into it. Will you spare it to me this evening? I think it is time now for lights to be extinguished."

Carol gave the book to her gladly, little thinking it would be many long days before he would see it again.

When Mrs. Mandeville returned to the drawing-room, the Rector was there. "Do you know anything of this book, Raymond?" she asked, giving it into his hand. "I found Carol reading it in bed--*Science and Health*." The frown which was habitually on the Rector's face deepened.

"Indeed I do," he said, "and I should like to do with every copy what I am going to do with this."

He walked over to the fireplace; his intentions were plain. Mrs. Mandeville caught hold of his arm.

"No, no, Raymond, you must not. The book was a present from Miss Desmond to Carol, and you have no right to destroy it, however strongly you may disapprove of his reading it."

"I do more than disapprove. I absolutely forbid him to read any more of it; the most unorthodox rubbish that has been published for centuries. The worst of it is, it has taken hold of some people, especially women, and they are carried away by it."

The Rector slipped the little book into his pocket. As he had not destroyed it, he meant to make sure there should be no chance of its falling again into Carol's hands. He, as well as Mrs. Mandeville, was the boy's legal guardian.

Mrs. Mandeville was sorry. She felt sure from the way Carol had spoken that the book was precious to him. Very gently, the next morning, she told him of his uncle's decision. She noted the quivering lips; the tears he was bravely trying not to shed.

"Dear boy, did you value it so much?" she said.

"Oh, Auntie!" The simple exclamation expressed more pain and regret than many words could have done.

"Darling, I am sorry; but we must believe that Uncle Raymond has good reasons for taking the book away. He says it is fearful heresy. You must not forget that your dear grandfather was a bishop, also your great-grandfather.

I could not tell you during how many generations there has always been at least one member of our family a dignitary of the Church."

"What does unorthodox mean, Auntie?"

"It means contrary to, or opposed to the teachings of our beloved church. Your dear father and mother were both good church people."

"Yes, Auntie; but that did not make Mummie better when she was so ill. The vicar often used to sit with her, and pray for her in church, but she was never better for it. When Cousin Alicia came and I was so ill, I began at once to get better. That little book, *Science and Health*, had taught her to understand the Bible, and God answered her prayers for me!"

"It was certainly a remarkable coincidence--your improving so quickly after Miss Desmond came; but it may have been the result of some fresh medicine the doctor was trying."

"Auntie, I was not taking any medicine. The first night Cousin Alicia came I slept till morning, and the next day I wanted something to eat. The nurses thought it was wonderful, because they had had such difficulty to get me to eat before. Then when they dressed the wounds on my hip every morning I used to scream so, some of the servants went where they could not hear me. In only one week I lost all the pain and I did not cry at all, and very soon one by one the wounds healed."

"It was very remarkable, dear. But do you associate your healing with the book which Uncle Raymond has taken away?"

"Why, Auntie, *Science and Health* is the Key to the Bible, and the Bible is the 'tree whose leaves are for the healing of the nations.' But people have not understood until they had that Key how to go to the Bible for healing. Cousin Alicia understood; that was why she was able to heal me."

"What you say seems very strange, Carol. If Uncle had not taken the book away, I should have liked to look into it. I expect he would refuse if I asked him to let me read it."

It did not occur to Mrs. Mandeville that she could obtain another copy of the book. The confiscated copy was not the only one to be had. Her conversation with Carol was interrupted just then. The same night when she went, as the evening before, to his bedroom, she found him sitting up in bed. He greeted her eagerly with the words:

"Auntie, I have been thinking."

"Dear boy, what have you been thinking?" She kissed the earnest, upturned face, and realized for the first time that he had a very beautiful countenance, so like, she thought, one of Murillo's child angels.

"I have been thinking, Auntie, of what you said about unorthodox. A good many years ago when Protestants were called heretics, they were unorthodox to the Church of Rome, were they not?"

"Certainly, dear."

"But Protestants are not called heretics now, are they?"

"I think we never hear them so spoken of now, dear, because there are more Protestants in England than Roman Catholics."

"Then, Auntie, when there are more Christian Scientists than other church people, *they* won't be called heretics."

"Will that ever be?" Mrs. Mandeville asked with a smile.

"Yes, Auntie; it must be, because Christian Scientists obey Jesus. All that he said and commanded in the New Testament, they try to carry out. He commanded his disciples to heal the sick."

"His disciples of that day, dear."

"But, Auntie, didn't he say: 'What I say unto you I say unto all.' If we love him we shall keep all his commandments. That is why I am sorry Uncle Raymond has taken away my *Science and Health*. I want to understand it like Cousin Alicia does; then some day, if I know little boys or girls ill like I was, I could heal them. It makes me so sorry now that I cannot study. I have written to Cousin Alicia to help me. I know she will. It has been so difficult all day to stand 'porter at the door of thought.' Such a lot of unkind thoughts would keep trying to get in. I know I must not let any of them in, and Cousin Alicia will help me to keep them out."

"I am afraid I do not quite understand, Carol."

"Don't you, Auntie? I have a little book that will explain. It is called 'At the Door.' Our mind is like a beautiful white mansion, and thoughts are like people who go in and out. If we let unkind thoughts pass in, all kind thoughts go away. Self-pity isn't at all a nice person, I have had such difficulty to keep him out all day, especially when I remembered that Father knew I was studying *Science and Health*, and he did not take it away from me."

"I will tell that to Uncle Raymond, dear, perhaps it will cause him to alter his decision."

"Thank you, Auntie; I know it will be all right. I have only to be patient. They have all gone away now, self-pity and indignation, and anger. If I keep my mansion so full of love, there will be no room for them to squeeze in, will there?"

"No, darling. Now go to sleep. I will take the little book down with me and read it."

Mrs. Mandeville remembered as she went downstairs her visit three years ago to Carol's home. Then she would have described him as a very spoilt child, making allowance for his illness, he was fretful, selfish, exacting. What had wrought such a marvellous change? The physical healing seemed slight in comparison.

CHAPTER IV.--A WELCOME LETTER.

Carol had been at the Manor a week before he received the eagerly expected letter from Cousin Alicia. Mrs. Mandeville brought it herself to the school-room for him.

"What a lucky little boy to get such a fat letter! I wonder the post-office didn't decline to bring it for a penny," she said smiling at his radiantly happy face. Then turning to Miss Markham, as lessons were about to commence, she asked:

"May he be excused for a little time, Miss Markham? I know he will like to take it to his room and read it quietly there."

"Oh, thank you, Auntie; thank you, Miss Markham," as the asked-for permission was quickly accorded, and he ran off with the treasured letter. Half an hour later he sought Mrs. Mandeville in her morning-room.

"Auntie, would you like to read my letter?"

"Indeed, dear, I should, if you would care for me to."

"Yes, Auntie. I would like you to read it very much. I knew Cousin Alicia would help me to understand. It has been just like having a talk with her. She always makes me feel happy."

He gave several sheets of closely written note paper into Mrs. Mandeville's hand.

"I must not be away any more lesson time, must I?"

He left the letter with her, and returned to the school-room. Mrs. Mandeville opened the pages, and read:

"WILLMAR COURT,

1.   DEVON.

"*My very dear Carol,*

"Until your first letter arrived it was difficult to realize that the train had carried you so far away from us. It seemed as if a spirit of sadness were creeping over the household, even the dogs and birds felt the subtle influence, and I had to dispel it by realizing that there can be no separation in Mind. Nothing can come between loving thoughts. I am as near to you in thought, and you to me as if these human arms enfolded you. It rejoiced me to read that you felt my thoughts like loving arms around you.

"Your first letter was awaited with eager expectation. I had to read parts to everyone. When Bob brought up your pony for his morning lump of sugar, I caught him brushing a tear away with his coat sleeve, as he asked, 'Will it be long before Master Carol comes home again?' I told him that was a question I could not answer, but possibly you might have the pony sent to Mandeville, and in that case he would no doubt accompany it.

"The bright happy strain of your first letter made me glad. Before I had time to answer it came the second in a minor key. After reading it, a thought that something was wrong tried hard to creep in. But I knew it could not be. 'Love governs and controls all events with unerring wisdom.' So I just took my hat and went for our favorite walk by the stream, to think things out. I seemed to feel your little hand in mine as I walked. I sat down on the old tree-stump, where you used to rest when you first began to walk; and do you remember the thrush which was always singing on the other side of the stream, how we used to think he sang a special song for you, and the words were, 'God is Love'? He was there on the same branch of the tree. I feel so sure now that it is the same bird. 'What message have you for Carol this morning?' I asked, and it seemed that the notes changed and the message came so clearly: 'All is right that seems most wrong.'

"Yes! I knew it I Of course it is! The bird flew off, and I walked on, thinking of a story I read many years ago. It was, I believe, an Eastern allegory. That story has often helped me; perhaps it will help you. I will tell it briefly. The King of a great country had many singing birds. They were to him as children, he loved them so. They were quite free to fly about the palace, or in the beautiful gardens of the palace, and when the King walked amongst them, they rested on his shoulder, or on his hand, when he held it out to them. There was one especial favorite--a little brown bird. It had not gay plumage like some of its companions, but its song delighted the King, and often he said: 'Sing--sing always.' One day the servants discovered the little brown bird was missing. Some one had stolen it from the palace. Word was brought to the King, and he quickly sent messengers all over his kingdom to discover where the bird was. It was not long before the place of confinement was known, and, to the surprise of everyone, the King left his little favorite in captivity. But he strictly commanded his messengers to watch over it, that no harm could come to it. Not a feather was to be ruffled.

"In partial darkness, beating its wings helplessly against the bars of the cage, the little brown bird yet remembered the King's command, 'Sing, sing always'; and every day it poured forth the song which the King loved. Strangers came from far to listen to the wondrous song of the little captive bird. Then, one day, the little bird looked up joyfully, at the sound of a well-known voice. The King himself had come to set the captive free. The cage door was quickly opened, and the bird flew forth, and rested on the King's shoulder, pouring forth such a song of joy as no one had ever heard before.

"'My priceless treasure!' the King exclaimed--the one note that was missing has come into your song.' And great was the King's joy as he carried the little brown bird back to his palace.

"I remember, when I read that story as a girl, being sorry that it ended there. I wanted to know that the wicked men were punished for stealing the bird, and that it was never separated again from the King who loved it so. But now I understand the story better, and the lesson it teaches. If the little bird had not been obedient to the King's command to sing always,--even when it was in captivity, it would never have learned that one missing note. And so, dear Carol, we have to learn under all circumstances and at all times that we are bidden to rejoice. The words are: 'Rejoice--again I say rejoice.'

"Having the book taken from you, as you do not yet understand the antagonism so many people manifest towards it, was doubtless a great surprise, when you owe so much to its teachings. But, dearie, you must not let any thoughts of injustice, or of something not quite right, creep in. The book will be returned to you one day. Love can always find a way. It will not be detained one moment after it is needful for you to have it again. You must put in practice, live up to, what you have already learned. You have only one step to take at present, and I think that step is 'obedience': cheerful, willing obedience, in every detail of your life. You see, dear Carol, we are told only one thing of the Master when he was a boy of your age: that is, 'He was subject [obedient] unto them.' Had it been necessary, we should have been told more. So from you, and all children, looking unto Jesus, to follow in his steps, one thing only is required--perfect obedience to those in authority over you, parents or guardians.

"Try to picture that humble home at Nazareth, and the carpenter's shop. We can never know the trials *he* had to bear in those early years, through those around him not comprehending his divine mission. From one verse in St. Matthew's Gospel we learn that taunts and gibes were thrown at him, because his spiritual birth was not understood. Yet those words have come down through all the centuries to inspire and help the young of all generations: *He was subject unto them.*

"The world has given an undue prominence to the wooden crucifix. The cross that Jesus carried for us he carried for 33 long years--working out each problem of life, and finally overcoming death, in order to show us the way to eternal life, then bidding us take up the cross--not the wooden crucifix--the cross of daily overcoming error with truth; and thus to follow him.

"When you are asked anything about Christian Science, and your own healing, if you are able, answer any questions quietly and courteously, but never obtrude the subject on anyone; or bring it forward voluntarily. Live Christian Science, dear Carol, not talk it. Be careful in all things to study your aunt's wishes; and as she evidently does not wish the subject mentioned to your cousins, do not mention it. Following in the steps that Jesus marked--perfect obedience--can never be denying Christ, and by perfect obedience, dear, you will understand, loving, willing, cheerful obedience, never allowing any thought of wrong or injustice to find a resting place in your consciousness.

"Write to me as often as you can, dear. Now that you have commenced regular lessons, you will not have so much spare time. Your letters will always be to me a joy, both to receive and to answer. I rejoice in my stewardship, taking care of this beautiful home for my dear boy. Colonel Mandeville wrote me that your dear father expressed his desire at the last that it should be so; and he himself also wrote a letter which was posted at Gibraltar. It had not yet reached me. I cannot understand it, as the letter from Colonel Mandeville which was evidently posted at the same time, bearing the Gibraltar post-mark, arrived, as you know, before you left. But we know it cannot be lost, although it is long over-due.

"Please convey my kind regards to Colonel and Mrs. Mandeville, and to yourself, dear Carol, unnumbered loving thoughts, from

COUSIN ALICIA.

"*P.S.* How I should like to see the sweet Rosebud and your other cousins!"

A very grave, thoughtful expression deepened on Mrs. Mandeville's face as she gathered the loose sheets of note paper together, and replaced them in the envelope. "Surely," she said, sotto voce, "if this is what Christian Science teaches, Raymond does not understand the book which he has taken away from Carol."

CHAPTER V.--QUIET DAYS.

The days which followed were quiet and uneventful, the peaceful, happy days which imperceptibly glide into weeks and months. Carol worked diligently at his lessons. He had so much lost time to make up.

Miss Markham was surprised at the progress he made. Whatever tasks she set him he mastered with ease, and never manifested fatigue or weariness. He was still so slight, even fragile, in appearance, she sometimes feared lest she was overtaxing his strength. Once, expressing fear lest this should be so, Carol answered lightly, "It is quite right, Miss Markham, the more work I do, the more I shall be able to do. Cousin Alicia is helping me every day."

"Miss Desmond is in Devonshire, Carol, how can she help you?"

"I am sorry, Miss Markham, I forgot you do not understand," he said.

He had been so perfectly obedient to Miss Desmond's wishes in never talking about Christian Science, that, excepting Mrs. Mandeville, no one remembered anything about it in connection with the boy. But, gradually, all the household were realizing there was something strangely different about the boy from other children. No one ever heard him complain of an ache or pain. No one ever heard him speak an unkind or angry word; and if, as sometimes, though seldom, amongst the Mandeville children, little dissensions or bickerings arose, if Carol was near, they passed as a ripple on water, and all was harmony and peace again.

Nurse loved to have him in the nursery. Miss Markham missed him when he was absent from the school-room. On one occasion when he was in the nursery a heavy box-lid was accidentally allowed to fall on Rosebud's fingers. The child screamed terribly with the pain, but before Nurse could do or say anything Carol seized her in his arms, and ran out of the room with her. In less than ten minutes he brought her back again, laughing merrily.

"Naughty fingers don't hurt Rosebud now," she said.

Nurse wondered, but, like Miss Markham, she did not understand.

It happened only a few days afterward that Mrs. Mandeville did not come as usual to the school-room immediately after breakfast, and everyone was sorrowful when it was known that Mother had one of her old nervous headaches. They knew it meant not seeing her for two or three days. She suffered terribly at times with her head, and had to lie in a darkened room, unable to bear the least noise. The children hushed their laughter and trod softly, though the school-room and nurseries were too far removed from Mrs. Mandeville's apartments for any sound to reach her.

After morning school, without saying a word to any one, Carol crept so noiselessly into the darkened room that Mrs. Mandeville was unaware of his presence, until he softly touched her with his hand, and said:

"Auntie, I am so sorry you are suffering. I do want to help you. Could I-- would you let me?"

"Dear boy, how sweet of you! I have frequently suffered with headaches like this for many years. Nothing can be done, dear. I can only be still and bear the pain until it passes."

Mrs. Mandeville spoke as if every word she uttered tortured her.

"Auntie, dear, won't you let me try to help you?"

"Do you mean, dear, you want to say a Christian Science prayer for me?"

"Yes, Auntie."

"Why, of course, darling, if you wish it. It is so very sweet of you!"

Carol softly kissed the hand she put out to him, and left the room, as noiselessly as he had entered, closing the door after him. He knew what pain was. He went straight to his own room and closed that door too. He did not leave his room until the gong sounded for the school-room dinner. His cousins exclaimed as he rejoined them,

"Wherever have you been all this time, Carol?"

But Carol did not say.

In the afternoon while the children were still seated round the tea-table, the school-room door opened, and Mrs. Mandeville entered the room. There was one vociferous exclamation of surprise and delight.

"Mother! Are you better?"

"I am quite better," she said, "I fell asleep. I must have slept a long time, and when I woke I felt quite well."

No one noticed the flush of joy that came to Carol's face. His hands were clasped, his eyes downcast as he silently breathed, "I thank Thee, my Father."

Before she left the room again, Mrs. Mandeville caressingly laid her hands on the boy's shoulders, and bent over to kiss his brow, but she did not allude to his visit to her room. Neither did he. Some sad days were to pass over the Manor household before Mrs. Mandeville acknowledged the help she had received.

Carol had not been long at Mandeville before he became almost as well acquainted with the villagers as his cousins. He frequently accompanied the three little girls and the second nurse, when they were deputed to carry a basket of good things to any house in the village where there was need. In this way he became acquainted with the village shoemaker, Mr. Higgs, who, in his younger days, had also acted as verger at the church. He explained to Carol the "rheumatiz" was so bad in his legs he hadn't been able to walk to church for months. He was often to be seen sitting at the open cottage door in the summer evenings, with an open Bible on his knees, his hands folded on it, for the print was too small for his failing eyesight.

Carol was thoughtful as he walked home. When Mrs. Mandeville paid her usual visit to his bedroom in the evening, she found him sitting up in bed, waiting for her. He was always awake when she came, but since she had desired him not to read in bed he never had a book in his hand. So often he greeted her with the words, "Auntie, I have been thinking."

"Well, darling, what have you been thinking about to-night?" she asked before he spoke, well knowing from his attitude that he had been thinking either of some pleasing or some perplexing subject.

"I have been thinking of something I can do, Auntie, if you will let me. It is only a very little thing, but if we do not begin with little things, we shall not be able some day to do big things, shall we? I so often think about Jesus when he was twelve years old, he said, 'I must be about my Father's business.' I am twelve years old, and God is my Father, too. I want to be about His business. When I was talking to old Mr. Higgs this morning, he told me he cannot walk to church now, and his eyes are so bad he cannot see to read the Bible. I thought I would like to go sometimes and read it to him, and help him to understand it. Would you let me, Auntie dear? It is such a little thing."

"Why, of course, dear; there can be no reason why you should not, if you wish to. I don't think Uncle Raymond can have any possible objection. Anyway, if I give you permission, that will be sufficient, will it not?"

"Oh, yes, Auntie; thank you so very much. May I go every Sunday evening?"

"Yes, dear; and perhaps it may not be such a little thing as you think."

Mrs. Mandeville thought of her own two boys. How different Carol was!

Neither of them would have dreamed of doing such a thing. "But," she mused, "his long illness has changed him."

"Auntie, I often try to picture Jesus in his humble home at Nazareth. I wish we knew more. When he returned with Joseph and Mary after the visit to the Temple, and was always obedient to them, I sometimes wonder if they kept him back from going about his Father's business, because they did not understand; and if he played on the hillsides with the other village boys, and no one knew until he was a man, that he was Jesus the Christ."

"There are many legends of his boyhood, dear, but they are only legends. We cannot accept anything except what is narrated in the Gospels. You must read Canon Farrar's 'Life of Christ.' That will help you to understand that the Apostles were, without doubt, divinely instructed to record so little of the boyhood of Jesus. There is a copy in the library. I will look it out for you."

"Thank you so much, Auntie. I shall be glad to read it."

Then clinging both arms round her neck, as she stooped to kiss him, he said:

"I do love your coming to my room like this, Auntie. I always keep awake till you come."

"I, too, enjoy our little talks, dear. You often give me a beautiful thought to take away with me: something I have not thought of before."

The boy lay awake a long time after Mrs. Mandeville left him, thinking joyfully of the work that had come to him, wondering how he should open the pages of that wonderful book, as they had been opened to him. "Teach me, Father-Mother God, the words of Truth that will help him," he prayed. Finally, he fell asleep with the words on his lips of the boy Samuel: "Speak, Lord, for Thy servant heareth."

CHAPTER VI.
FIRST WORK IN THE VINEYARD.

"Would you like me to read to you for a little while this evening, Mr. Higgs? My aunt has given me permission, if you would like me to," Carol asked modestly as he entered the old man's cottage the following Sunday evening. Mr. Higgs was seated as usual at the open door, watching the villagers pass by on their way to church.

"Thank you kindly, young gentleman. I'll be glad to hear some of the words of the Book. I just keep it close by me. It don't seem Sunday without. But my eyes fail me, and I just sit and ponder over some of the Psalms I can well remember. After the service sometimes a neighbor'll pop in and tell me the text Rector's been preaching about. A mighty fine preacher is Rector, but often I used to say to my Missus--she's dead and gone these five years-- his thoughts are like birds, they fly over our heads, and we don't seem able to lay hold of them. If he'd just tell us something simple to help us day by day. I'd be glad now if I could remember some of the sermons I've listened to, year in, year out. But there, it's all gone, and I've got no more understanding of the Bible than when I was a boy. It's ower late to think about it now, and me turned seventy."

"I have been taught to understand the Bible. I should like to teach you what I have been taught. Then, when you understand, you would lose your rheumatism."

"*Lose my rheumatism!*" The old man repeated the words in the utmost astonishment.

"Why, yes, of course you would," Carol said with that wonderfully sweet smile which won all hearts. "I had hip-disease; but I lost it."

"Well, now, young gentleman, I can say with absolute truth that I have never been told that before--no, *never!* though I've been a regular church attendant since I was a little choir boy, and never left off going till the joints in my old legs grew so stiff I couldn't walk. It'd want a lot of faith, sir, to believe that just reading the Bible would make 'em lissom again."

"Faith comes with understanding. There is another book; it is called *Key to the Scriptures*. I haven't a copy of that book now, but I can remember so much of it, I shall be able to help you to understand the Bible perhaps a little better. We will commence with the first chapter of Genesis."

"Yes, now; I remember that chapter pretty well. I learnt it at Sunday School sixty years ago, and I've never quite forgotten it. I could repeat verses straight off now."

"And has it never helped you all through your life?"

"Well, no. I can't say that chapter has. I have found comfort sometimes from the Psalms. 'The Lord is my Shepherd, I shall not want,' I have often turned to when we'd a growing family and work was slack."

"Let me read the chapter now and then we will talk about it."

The boy opened the Bible, and slowly with an impressiveness which the old man had never before heard, he read the first chapter of Genesis, and three verses of the second chapter. He read as one reads words that are very familiar and understandable.

"*Thus the heavens and the earth were finished, and all the host of them, and God saw everything that He had made, and behold it was very good.*" He repeated the words from memory, looking with a kindly smile at the old man, as he asked the question: "If God looked upon everything which He had created, and declared it very good--where do the things come from that are not good? Who created them?"

"Well now, young sir, that is a question I'm not prepared to answer. I can only say like that little black girl in the story, "spose they growed'."

"But everything must grow from something, mustn't it? Every tree and plant has its own seed. God created every living creature after its kind, and bade it be fruitful and multiply. So you see everything good was created by the Word of God. Is rheumatism good?"

"'Deed no, young gentleman! It's cruel bad."

"So is hip-disease. It's very, very 'cruel bad,' and because it is the opposite of good it was not amongst the things which God 'beheld.' Our dear Heavenly Father did not create poor suffering little children maimed with hip-disease, and sometimes blind. He created them in His own image and likeness, and God could not be suffering sometimes with one disease, sometimes with another, so that His image and likeness could have it too, could He? See, if I hold my hand up so it casts a shadow on the wall, that is an exact image or likeness of my hand, is it not? Now if I just hold something--only a slip of paper between my hand and the reflection, the reflection is deformed, isn't it? But my hand is not affected by it. So when we are bound by any cruel disease, there is something between God and His image and likeness, something that was never created by Him--was never created at all. It is only a shadowy mist--a belief: and we have to get rid of it, by knowing its unreality. We have to know that because we are

God's children, His spiritual creation, we must be perfect, even as He is perfect. Jesus came to teach people this. He said, 'Be ye therefore perfect, even as your Father in Heaven is perfect.' But, my cousin says, the world has been slow to learn the lesson. Sin and disease will disappear from our midst just as soon as we do learn it. When she came to me, and I was very ill, she taught me that nothing was real except what God had created, and pronounced good, and He never created hip-disease. Because she understood this so clearly, and taught me to understand it, I soon began to get better. I should like to help you to understand it, so that you would lose your rheumatism. I think I have stayed as long as I had permission to-night. Would you like me to come again next Sunday?"

"'Deed, and I would, young gentleman."

"My name is Carol," the boy said simply.

"Thank 'ee, Master Carol, you've given me something to think about, I shan't forget during the week."

"I should like to teach you the Scientific Statement of Being. It is in that book I told you of, which explains the Bible. If you would learn it, and try to realize it, it would help you so much.'

"My mem'ry 's none of the best now, but I'll try," the old man said regretfully.

"Perhaps it will be better for me to write it for you in large writing, so that you can read it until you know it. I will bring it with me next week. These are the words: 'There is no life, truth, intelligence, nor substance in matter.' He repeated the words gravely and slowly to the end, the old man gazing at him the while with wondering eyes. The sun was setting; the crimson light streamed through the lattice window upon the boy's upturned face, so sweet, so grave, so loving, and so earnest.

"The words seem difficult to understand at first," he said, "but you will soon grow to love them. It is the truth which Jesus promised should make us free. It has made me free. It will make you free."

CHAPTER VII.--"I KNOW."

Carol bounded through the park with a light, joyous step. On reaching the Manor House, he would have gone straight to his aunt, but there were visitors with her. So he rejoined his cousins in the school-room.

"Where ever have you been, Carol?" they questioned, as he entered.

"Somewhere Auntie gave me permission to go," he replied quietly.

Miss Markham looked at the boy's beaming face, and she too wondered. He had been absent from the Scripture lesson, which she, and sometimes Mrs. Mandeville, gave the children every Sunday evening. She felt a little remorse that she had been conscious during the lesson of a feeling of relief, on account of the boy's absence. Carol so often asked a question in a quiet, thoughtful manner, which she was unable to answer: and the question would often recur to her afterwards. She had an intuition that the boy had a firmer grasp of spiritual truths than she herself possessed. Many times she would have liked to discuss a subject with him. But Mrs. Mandeville had warned her that the boy had been taught much that was unorthodox, she therefore refrained from discussion.

Though it was much later than usual, Carol was wide awake when Mrs. Mandeville came to his room that night. She had found all the other children fast asleep.

"Auntie, I did want to tell you, I had a very happy time with Mr. Higgs. He's such a nice, interesting old man. I was able to tell him so much that he had never thought about before. Thank you again for letting me go. He will like me to go next Sunday--I may--mayn't I?"

"Of course, dear; as it seems to make you so happy; and I am sure it must be very nice for Mr. Higgs to have you read to him, as he is so troubled with rheumatism. But you must really settle down to sleep now, Carol. You have no idea how late it is."

"Yes, Auntie, I shall soon be asleep, I wanted to tell you first. I feel so happy now, I can say one verse of Mrs. Eddy's beautiful hymn to-night which commences;

'My prayer some daily good to do,
'To thine for Thee;'

"Cousin Alicia used to sing it to me every night when I was ill. I loved it so much, because its measures *did* bind the power of pain. Often I had fallen asleep before she came to the end."

"You must repeat all the hymn to me some time, Carol, I shall like to hear it."

"Yes, Auntie, in the morning. I have been thinking whilst I was waiting for you to come that when we want to do something for Truth very, very much, Love finds the way. When I am a man, I shall want, more than anything in all the world, just to do what Jesus said, those that loved him were to do, 'Go ye into all the world, preach the Gospel, and heal the sick.' I cannot help remembering there are so many little children lying now, just as I used to lie, always in pain; and they could be healed, just as I was healed, if there were more people who understood what Jesus meant by 'The truth shall make you free."

"And you are quite sure, Carol, it is that which has made you free?"

"Oh, Auntie, dear, I can never let even the tiniest thought of doubt creep up and make me question that. I *know*. When Uncle Raymond read in church last Sunday 'I know that my Redeemer liveth,' I felt I wanted to stand up and tell all the people *because* He liveth, I am well. That is 'knowing.' I do long for the time to come when I shall be able to tell them so, and I can give all my time and my money to spread the glad tidings, to fight for Truth."

"Maybe there is a great work, a great future before you, dear boy, surely the instrument has been prepared in a fierce fire, and has come forth strong for the battle. Now, good-night, and God bless you, darling." He clasped both his arms round her neck, holding her tightly, as in earlier years he used to cling to his mother.

CHAPTER VIII.
A SECOND VISIT TO THE COTTAGE.

The next Sunday evening when Carol entered the shoemaker's cottage, he was not alone as before.

"This is my daughter, Mrs. Scott, Master Carol, and her little girl," he said to Carol. "We thought, maybe, you wouldn't object if she listened to the reading too. She cannot often go to church, because the little girl has been subject to epilepsy since she was two years old. She's just turned eight now. I told her mother what you told me last Sunday, and she'll be right glad to hear more."

"That I shall, Master Carol. I know something of hip-disease, and if you could be cured of that, I'm sure my little girl could be cured of the fits."

"Why, of course she could. You will be able to help her ever so much only by knowing that God never created fits; they belong to the mist which we read about in the second chapter of Genesis. I am going to read that chapter to Mr. Higgs to-night. Then you'll understand. I will begin at the fourth verse, because the first three verses belong really to the first chapter, which is an account of the first creation, when God made everything that was made and it was spiritual and perfect. No one could ever alter or undo God's perfect work; it remains, and always will remain, perfect. When we understand this, and realize it, the mist will disappear, and all the things which belong to the mist--sin, disease, and death."

Father and daughter looked at the boy with wonder and perplexity. Opening the Bible he read:

"These are the generations of the heavens and the earth when they were created in the day that the Lord God made the earth and the heavens." He continued to the end of the chapter. "Now do you see how different this account of creation is from the first?" he asked. "Who was the Lord God who took the dust of the ground and formed man over again, after God had already created him, and pronounced His work very good?"

The old man shook his head, "I can only say, as I said last Sunday, Master Carol, in all the sermons I've listened to that has never been explained to me. I don't think I should have let it slip, if it had. It's just the first time I've ever known there were two creations."

"There were not really two creations, though it reads as if there were, because there are not two creators. The sixth verse explains it, 'There went up a mist from the earth and watered the whole face of the ground.' That mist covered everything which God-Spirit had created--all the host of them; birds, beasts, and flowers, mountains, seas, lakes, rivers, even man: God's own image and likeness. Because the mist is over everything we do not see the world and man as they really exist. So people have come to believe that God made man from the dust; for the mist that is spoken of is not a mist like we see rising from the sea, or in the fields of an evening. It means false belief, misunderstanding of God and His spiritual creation. But, my cousin has told me, there is a woman in America who once caught a glimpse of God's real creation as she was passing through the death valley. And that one glimpse restored her to health. Then she devoted her whole life to learn more of the truth that she might teach others how to see through the mist, and to shake off their old beliefs. She has written a book called *Science and Health* with *Key to the Scriptures*, which explains all that she has discovered. Simply reading and studying that book has made hundreds of people well."

"Where could we get a copy of it, Master Carol? I'd like to know for my little girl's sake," Mrs. Scott asked.

"I do not quite know, but there are Christian Science churches in London. If you were to write there perhaps someone would tell you. I wish I had a copy to lend you. I have written the Scientific Statement of Being from memory. I am sure it will help you. I am trying to realize it for you, and for the little girl. Think always of that first chapter of the Bible. In the beginning God created everything that was created, and it was very good. None of the things we want to get rid of could be included in God's *very good*, could they? Jesus came to teach men to understand God better, and he said, 'that which is born of the Spirit is spirit.' So all that came from God and all that still comes is spiritual. If you could quite realize this, Mr. Higgs, you would soon lose your rheumatism. I am only telling you what has been told me so many times; and I know it is true, because I was very ill when my cousin used to teach me, and I grew better as I began to understand. She helped me, because she saw me always as God's perfect child, and knew that He had never created hip-disease, therefore it never was created; it belonged to the mist, and it would disappear under the light of Truth as hoar frost disappears when the sun shines upon it."

"It is wonderful and strange what you are telling us, Master Carol, I've never heard the like before, but somehow I can't doubt it. I call to mind what the Bible says, 'Out of the mouths of babes and sucklings God ordains strength.' I'd dearly love the girl to be free from those dreadful fits. My rheumatiz is very bad, but I'm an old man, and can't expect to 'scape one o' the signs of old age."

"But you must not expect. You must know that it is not a sign of old age in God's man. You must always remember the man whom God created in His own image and likeness."

"I've heard those words many times before, Master Carol, but somehow they never seemed to come home to me as you put it. Why, of course I ought not to suffer with rheumatiz if I *am* God's image and likeness. But what about all the poor dwarfed and stunted creatures that are crippled from infancy? There's a little hunchback in the village. He was dropped when he was a baby, and his back grew crooked, so that it's a hump now. How can he be God's image and likeness?"

"The hunchback is not the likeness of God, but the real child--the spiritual child is, and God sees His child as He created it." The boy put his hand over his eyes a moment, realizing that of himself he was not telling these simple-minded people anything. Then he said:

"Suppose a great sculptor carved a beautiful statue out of a block of marble. Before he began his work, he would have in his mind the form he wished the marble to take. Gradually, as he worked at it, the marble would become what his thought of it was. Then one day he would see it finished and perfect--just what he intended it to be. Then he would work no more at it. Afterwards, suppose some one came by, and took clay and mixed it with water into a paste, and then daubed the beautiful statue all over, till the limbs looked crooked, and the beauty of the face was spoiled. But it wouldn't be really spoiled, would it? The statue would still be the work of the great sculptor, finished and perfect; the clay and the marble would be quite separate and distinct. Nothing could make them one. So when we read the chapter I have just read to you--the Lord God took the dust of the ground and made man--God's man was already made, finished and perfect, and the dust, like the clay, could only seem to hide the perfect creation. But we have to know this and to realize it, if we are to get rid of the dust, and the clay, and the mist. When my cousin was explaining all this to me one day, she said, 'It is not known how or when the belief in a Lord God who made man of dust arose; but from that false belief came sin, sorrow, disease, and death. Jesus came to teach us the way back to God; to teach us to see ourselves as the children of God, not of the dust; and he said all who believed in him, in what he taught, would never see death.' The day will come, my cousin said, when all men will so believe in Jesus the Christ, and will so understand and realize that God is their Father, that death will be overcome. Every case of sin and disease which is healed by this knowledge--by the Truth--is bringing that day nearer."

The look of bewilderment deepened on the old man's face. Surely, the boy was throwing a different light upon words with which he had been familiar all his life. "We'll think over what you've told us, Master Carol--me and my daughter. It sort o' goes to me that it's true."

Again the words came to him, "Out of the mouth of babes and sucklings."

The church clock chimed the half-hour. Carol stood up to go. "The time has gone so quickly. I must not stay longer now. I will come again next Sunday, and all the week will you try to know that God's work was finished and perfect in the beginning, and everything that seems to have been added to it--rheumatism and fits--has no right to be?"

"We will, Master Carol, we'll just think of the marble statue and the clay. It will help us."

"I will hold the right thought for you and the little girl, and I know that soon you will find that both the afflictions, which seem so real, belong to the mist."

CHAPTER IX.--"IT IS THE TRUTH."

Carol faithfully kept his appointment on the following Sunday. His cousins ceased to inquire, though not to wonder, what became of him every Sunday evening, and once appealed to Mrs. Mandeville for information. She smilingly replied, "It is a little secret between Carol and me. Perhaps you will be told some time, but not just yet."

As Carol entered the cottage, Mr. Higgs rose from his seat, and stood upright.

"Master Carol," he exclaimed in a voice of suppressed excitement, "it is the Truth, the blessed Truth you've told us. I can't say I've lost my rheumatics entirely, for the joints are like rusty hinges that want a lot o' oiling after being idle so long; but I've just been free from pain all the week; and my little grand-daughter hasn't had one fit all the week."

"No, Master Carol, she has not," Mrs. Scott added. "I won't say she has never gone a whole week without one before, but for the last twelve months I don't think she has, until this week."

"Try not to remember anything that has been. Think it was all a dream, and she is awakening from it. I had a very cruel dream once, but I have awakened from it. God's children must cling very closely to Him, then nothing can hurt them. It is when shadowy fears come between God and His image and likeness that dreadful things seem to happen to us."

Mr. Higgs and Mrs. Scott did not understand yet how the boy had all the week been working for them--fighting error with the sword of Truth.

"I want to read a chapter from the New Testament this evening," Carol said, opening the Bible. "It is always a favorite chapter, but one verse, my cousin said, seemed never to have impressed people as applicable to the present day. Yet the words are so simple. I will read the chapter first, then we'll talk about that one verse."

He read the 14th chapter of St. John from the 1st verse to the last, then asked quietly, "Do you remember that Jesus once said, 'Heaven and earth shall pass away, but my words shall never pass away'?"

"Yes, Master Carol. I remember those words well."

"Then is there not a verse in the chapter I have just read which seems as if Jesus' words *had* failed?" The old man looked puzzled.

"I can't say that I know what you are alluding to, Master Carol."

"I will read it again. It is the 12th verse. 'Verily, verily, I say unto you, he that believeth on me, the works that I do shall he do also, and greater works than these shall he do, because I go unto my Father.' What were the works that Jesus did? Was it not healing the sick, cleansing the lepers, raising the dead, feeding the hungry? Well, if no one can do these works to-day, his word has failed or else no one has sufficient faith (faith may sometimes mean understanding). Many centuries rolled by, and the sick were not healed, nor the lepers cleansed, in Jesus' name. But now we know his words never failed. It was the faith or understanding of those who thought they believed in him which failed; for the sick are being healed now, and the lepers cleansed."

"It is very wonderful as you put it, Master Carol. I can't say it has ever been explained like that to me before."

"Is it not very simple?" Carol asked.

"Why, yes. It has always seemed to me the Master's words were very simple, a child could understand them. But when you come to the Epistles, and the creeds of the Church, there's many things that I have never been able to understand; and often the sermons I've listened to puzzled me more than the texts."

"In the 15th verse Jesus says, 'If ye love me, keep my commandments.' Jesus did not give many commandments to his followers. He told them many things, but of strict commandments he gave only a few. One was, 'Go into all the world, preach the Gospel and heal the sick.' If you had a son, and you commanded him to do two things and he did only one, and left the other alone, would you be pleased with him? Would he be obedient to your commands?"

"Certainly I shouldn't be pleased with him, and I'd soon let him know that, if he didn't do all I commanded, he needn't do anything."

"Yes, but Jesus just makes it a test of love. He says so gently, 'If ye love me, keep my commandments.' To those who keep all his commandments he will one day say, 'Well done, good and faithful servant,' I do hope that some day he will say those words to me."

"I'm right sure he will, Master Carol. It is just wonderful the way you are helping an old man to understand. It amazes me that a boy of your years should have such an understanding."

"Oh, please don't think I am telling you anything of myself. It has all been explained to me many times. I am only telling you what has been told me. I wish my cousin could talk to you. She would help you much better than I can. But we must not withhold what we have because some one else has more, must we? We must hand on the good tidings as well as we are able."

"That's it, Master Carol. Maybe I'll do a little that way myself later on."

"Yes, I am sure you will, but don't talk about your rheumatism being better just yet. Wait until the evil is quite cast out. When I come next week I will explain to you how we learn in *Science and Health* that God gave man dominion, and what God has given can never be taken away. God says His word shall never return unto Him void. When He decreed anything, it was forever. You could not think of the sun, moon, or stars moving out of their appointed courses, could you? It is only man who seems to have wandered from his native sphere. We have to learn that this is not so; we have not really lost the dominion which God gave His children in the beginning. St. John says, 'Now are we the sons of God; and it doth not yet appear what we shall be, but we know that when He shall appear we shall be like Him, for we shall see Him as He is.' That verse helped me so much when I was ill. I learned I had not to die to become a son of God. God is my Father here and now, and God's child ought not to believe a lie. It was a lie that evil could have power over me, and bind me. It is a lie that evil can have power over you, and bind you. If you acknowledge God as your Father, God's child should not go along believing he has rheumatism, should he?"

"Thank you, Master Carol. I'll take hold of that. I can understand it. I wish Rector would talk to us sometimes like this. I know it is all in the Bible, yet it never came home to me before."

Mrs. Scott listened attentively to all the boy was telling her father, but made no remark. Her little girl was sitting in the porch nursing her doll, crooning a lullaby. Carol left them with the promise to come again next Sunday.

CHAPTER X.--AN UNEXPECTED ENCOUNTER.

With thoughts so joyous and uplifted, Carol's feet scarcely seemed to touch the springy turf of the park as he returned to the Manor. The uplifting joy, unlike anything that earth can give, which comes from the consciousness that work done for, and in the Master's name, is accepted of him, was his; the promised signs following.

He did not see Mrs. Mandeville until she paid her usual visit to his bedroom.

His young face was radiant with joy and happiness. "Auntie," he said, "Mr. Higgs is beginning to understand; and he is losing his rheumatism."

Mrs. Mandeville smiled. There was so much love and tenderness in her smile the incredulity was not apparent. She put a loving arm around him, drawing the boy closer to her.

"Is that what you have been thinking to-night, dear?"

"Not altogether, Auntie. I have been thinking of what it means by the words, 'The mind that was in Christ.' That was what I was reading when I came to bed. If we are to have that Mind, we should understand what it is. But, Auntie, I can't get any farther than *love*: the mind that was in Christ was love. God is Love, and Jesus said, 'I and my Father are one.' So, Auntie, when our hearts are filled with love for the poor and afflicted and sorrowing, it is the Christ mind that comes to us. Because Jesus loved all who came to him, he was able to heal them. He said, 'I can of myself do nothing, it is the Father that worketh in me. He doeth the works.' Jesus was a perfect mirror, reflecting the love which is God. That is why he said, 'They that have seen me have seen my Father also.' Cousin Alicia explained this once to me, but I did not quite understand it at the time. I see so clearly now. When we reflect love as Jesus did, we shall be able to do the works that he did. I often wonder, Auntie, why Uncle Raymond and all the clergy who preach the Gospel don't help people when they are ill. It is not being obedient, is it?"

Mrs. Mandeville's face was grave.

"Ought I not to question this, Auntie?"

"Perhaps it would be better not, dear, until you are older. I do not understand myself. It is a subject I never seriously considered until you came to us. Now I think I must say good-night, my little lie-awake."

"I always fall asleep soon after I have said 'good-night' to you, Auntie."

"That is right, darling. I do enjoy our little talks; they are very sweet and helpful to me, Carol."

Then, after a long, loving embrace, she left him, a grave, thoughtful, but happy expression on her face.

The following Saturday morning after breakfast the three little girls told Carol, with delight, that they were going to the home farm in the afternoon, and begged him to go with them. Carol promised. He never refused to go anywhere or to do anything when Rosebud asked him. It was different with Percy and Frank. They were always too busy.

Carol knew how great a delight a visit to the farm was to the little girls, where each had a special pet of her own which the farmer's wife kindly took care of for them. Carol had visited the farm once before, and was almost as interested as the little girls in the animals and poultry yard. The schoolroom children had grown out of the interest they once had in visiting the farm.

Saturday being a school holiday, the boys were at home all day. After lunch Percy said:

"I say, Carol, some fellows are coming this afternoon; we are going to have a game at rounders. You can manage that. Will you come?"

Carol was never asked to join in a game at cricket or football, as his uncle and aunt feared it would not be good for him. "I am sorry, Percy; I cannot. I promised Rosebud and Sylvia to go with them to the farm this afternoon."

Percy turned impatiently away. He was annoyed. Carol caught the muttered words: "Milk-sop prefers a walk with the babies."

He was not versed in school-boy slang, but naturally felt it was an opprobrious epithet applied to himself. A crimson flush rose to his face. On the way to the farm, he asked Jane, the second nurse, who accompanied them:

"Can you tell me what milk-sop means, Jane?"

"Well, Master Carol, it's what school-boys call one another, sometimes. But it's not a nice word. I suppose it means something of a coward."

Carol fell behind. The crimson flush returned and dyed his cheeks again. "Percy did not mean it. He spoke without thinking. He forgot I am a soldier's son. *I am not angry.* I will not let you in!"

"Were you speaking, Master Carol?" Jane asked.

"I was only telling Mrs. Anger and Mr. Anger, and a lot of little Angers, there is no room for them in my mansion. Love is there, and cannot be driven away."

"You do say such funny things, Master Carol," Jane remarked.

"But there is nothing funny in that, Jane. You see our mind is our mansion, and if we keep it filled with loving thoughts, angry thoughts cannot creep in. Some angry thoughts were just trying to force their way in, and I had to tell them there was no room."

Still Jane smiled, but she, as everyone else at the Manor, loved the gentle boy, who had what seemed to them such strange thoughts.

A messenger always appeared to go in advance and tell the farmer's wife when the little ladies might be expected. She never failed to have such a lovely tea spread on a snowy white tablecloth, and her best china gracing the table. Tea in the farm kitchen was quite different from the usual nursery tea at home. Such delicious scones and tea-cakes! (It really would not have pleased cook to hear the praise bestowed upon them, as if she did not make quite as good.)

After tea they went around the farmyard to inspect their pets. A little gosling, quite tame and friendly, was chosen for Carol's especial pet. The hour, which was all nurse had allowed them, passed very quickly, and they started on the homeward walk. They had not gone far when a drizzling rain began. Jane then suggested the advisability of crossing a field which would shorten the distance considerably. When they came to the field, she was surprised to find the gate fastened.

"This gate is generally open. I wonder why it is padlocked to-day, but it is not too high to get over. If you climb over first, Master Carol, I can lift Rosebud over to you."

Carol soon mounted the five-barred gate, and landed safely on the other side, then received one by one Rosebud, Estelle, and Sylvia, from Jane's arm, as she lifted them over. They had walked about two hundred yards when Jane stood still in an agony of fright, as an animal, which had been lying unperceived in a distant corner of the field, rose up and came towards them with a loud bellow.

"Oh, Master Carol! What shall we do? It's the bull! He's a terror! I've heard of him. He's a tosser!"

"Don't be frightened, Jane. Just walk quietly. The bull won't hurt us, if we are not frightened."

Jane caught Rosebud in her arms, and with Estelle and Sylvia clinging to either side, walked as quickly as she dared towards the stile on the other side of the field. Fortunately, it was a stile easier to mount than the five-barred gate had been. It was but the work of a moment and the three little girls were lifted safely to the other side. Then, Jane turned to look for Carol. He had walked only a third of the distance, keeping always between the bull and his cousins, and now he stood face to face with the animal, a few yards only between them. Another low bellow, and then the animal bent his head to the ground, prepared for a spring.

"Run, run, Master Carol," Jane screamed. It was a fatal appeal. The mesmerism of fear seized Carol. He turned to look after his cousins. The next instant he was on the horns of the animal, tossed high in the air, as if he had been no heavier than an India-rubber ball. Mercifully, he fell on the other side of the hedge, which divided that field from the next. With a roar of baffled rage, the animal stampeded the field, seeking to toss his victim a second time.

CHAPTER XI.--PERCY'S REMORSE.

The three little girls set up a piteous cry of "Carol," "Carol." Jane was speechless, only wringing her hands in her extremity. What could she do? It was half a mile to return to the farm for help, and a mile to the nearest lodge belonging to the Manor; and there was no house between. She could not see where Carol had fallen. But she knew it was over the hedge into the next field. She feared the infuriated animal would force its way through. Though she could not in any way protect him, it seemed terrible to go from the place, even to get help, and leave him there. Many moments were lost in her frenzied attempts to force an entrance into the field from the lane. It was in vain. The thick, high hedge was impregnable. She called again and again to Carol to speak, to answer her, but there was no response. It seemed an eternity before there was the welcome sound of a horse's hoofs in the lane, which drew nearer until a stanhope came in sight, containing Colonel Mandeville, a friend, and a groom.

The three little girls cried: "Daddy, Daddy, the bull has tossed Carol!"

Colonel Mandeville sprang from the vehicle on the instant, scarcely understanding what the children said. Their distress was evident. That was sufficient. Jane then tried to explain.

"We were crossing the field, sir. I did not know the bull was there. He has tossed Master Carol over the hedge into this field, and we cannot get at him."

Colonel Mandeville uttered one low, sad exclamation.

"Where is the entrance into the field?" he asked.

"There is a gate into it from the field where the bull is. Oh, please, sir, it isn't safe; the bull is awfully enraged," she added, as Colonel Mandeville walked towards the stile.

He turned to say to the groom: "Follow me," and to his friend: "Manton, drive to the village and bring Dr. Burton along. I fear we shall want him." To Jane he said briefly: "Take the children home."

Then he mounted the stile, and entered the field, a gun in his hand, which the groom had handed him from the stanhope. The gentlemen had been shooting. The bull was standing in the middle of the field. He sprang towards the fresh intruder with a bellow. Colonel Mandeville pointed his gun; there was a report, and the next instant the beast rolled over on his side, dead. The groom then followed his master. They had a little difficulty in opening the gate into the next field, but succeeded at last, and were able to get in.

Under the shadow of the hedge Carol was lying--still, motionless.

Colonel Mandeville knelt beside him.

"Carol, Carol," he said softly, but there was no response. "Go to the farm as quickly as you can. Tell them to improvise an ambulance. Bring it along. Lose not a moment," he said to the groom.

Then he knelt on the ground, trying again to awake the boy to consciousness: "My poor wife, how will she bear this?" he said to himself, knowing well that Carol was as dear to her as her youngest born, the Rosebud of the family. The signs of life were so faint, he could not hope the boy would ever regain consciousness.

Dr. Burton was fortunately at home. In an inconceivably short time he arrived on the scene; and the groom returned with an ambulance, followed by the farmer, his wife, and some of the men, all anxious to give any assistance they could.

Dr. Burton and Colonel Mandeville very tenderly lifted Carol on to the ambulance, a faint moan was the only sign of life, but all were glad to hear even that. Dr. Burton would not make any examination until they could lay him on a bed, and cut off his clothes.

There was no question of breaking the news gently to Mrs. Mandeville; she was returning from a drive as the little girls reached the gates. They ran to her sobbing broken-heartedly.

She was very calm, but her face grew deadly white, and wore again the strained expression which had been so frequent during the sad days of the war. She could not remain inactive, and walked to meet the sad procession.

As soon as Colonel Mandeville saw her, he advanced quickly to her side, and turned her steps homeward. He would not let her see the boy as he lay on the ambulance, looking so like death.

Only Colonel Mandeville was with Dr. Burton when he made the critical examination. There were no broken bones, he said, but added that there are things worse to deal with than broken bones, and hinted gravely at concussion of the brain and spinal congestion. There were two terrible bruises where he had been caught on the bull's horns. He could not hold out any hope to them, but desired a second opinion, and a telegram was at once despatched to a great London physician, who, it was calculated, would be able to reach Mandeville that night if he caught the evening express. Then Mrs. Mandeville took her place by the bedside. She could do nothing, only watch in tearful silence the pallid face that had become so dear to her, lying so still, so calm, it seemed at times the lips were breathless. The reply telegram came quickly. Sir Wilfrid would be able to catch the evening express which would stop at Mandeville by request. He would reach the Manor about ten o'clock.

Not until the physician's arrival, when he and Dr. Burton held a consultation together, did Mrs. Mandeville leave the bedside. She then retired to her own room for a little time. Miss Markham came to her there, begging her to go and speak to Percy. "His grief," she said, "is quite uncontrollable. I have done all I can to comfort him. But nothing I can say seems to touch him." Mrs. Mandeville went at once to Percy's room. He had thrown himself undressed on his bed, and was sobbing hysterically, as she entered the room.

"Percy, my dear boy, you must not grieve like this."

As soon as he was aware it was his mother beside him, he flung his arms round her neck.

"Oh, Mother, I can never, never, be happy again if Carol dies. If he had not been there with them, the bull would have tossed my little sisters. Jane said he stood between them and the bull. He is the bravest boy, and I--I--called him a--a--" He could not repeat the word he had so lightly, thoughtlessly uttered a few hours previously.

"If only I could tell him I did not mean it, and ask him to forgive me, Mother. Oh! won't he ever be able to speak to me again?"

"Dear Percy, I hope so. Sir Wilfrid Wynne is with him now, and everything possible will be done for him. I am sure, darling, he would not like you to grieve like this. He always has such loving thoughts of others." The remembrance of all his gentleness and loving thought for others was too much for Mrs. Mandeville. Clasping her boy closely to her, she wept with him. Heaven was still to her a locality, and death the gateway to it; and Carol had always seemed so very near to the Kingdom of Heaven.

All the household awaited with cruel suspense the great man's verdict, trusting to him, forgetful that human skill had failed the boy once before in his hour of need, forgetful of that friend in Devonshire who loved him as her own son. No message had been sent to her.

CHAPTER XII.--THE PHYSICIAN'S VERDICT.

Sir Wilfrid Wynne gave his verdict, and it was almost a repetition of what Dr. Burton had said. He could do nothing. There was little hope he would regain consciousness. If he did, it would be but a passing flash before the end. He might linger in his present condition twenty-four hours or longer; and he might pass away any moment without a struggle. It would be cruel to wish him to live; the shock to the spine had been so great, if he lived, he would inevitably lose the use of his lower limbs. Sir Wilfrid was grieved; he had known the boy's father. He would gladly have remained, had there been any hope of doing anything for him. He took his departure by motor-car to catch the mail train at a junction ten miles distant.

Mrs. Mandeville returned to her place by the bedside, calm and still, after her paroxysm of weeping. Colonel Mandeville was with her, and presently the Rector came into the room.

"Raymond, pray for him," Mrs. Mandeville said. "He is in God's hands. No human power can help him."

They all knelt and the Rector prayed aloud. He did not petition for the boy's life to be spared. He humbly asked that the hearts of those who loved him might be submissive to God's all-wise decree. "Thy will be done," was the dominant note of the prayer. When they rose from their knees, there was an expression on Mrs. Mandeville's face which no one had ever seen before. The prayer had not helped her: it was not submission nor resignation in any degree which had come to her. She turned to the Rector.

"I do not believe it, Raymond. This is *not* God's will. God could not order anything so cruel to befall a child, so loving and dutiful--whose faith in God's loving care of him has always been so beautiful to me to witness. Could I, who know only human love, suffer anything like this to befall my little Rosebud, or any of my children? Is human love more pitiful and compassionate than divine love? This dear boy could easily have saved himself; he stood between the cruel beast and my little girls. All three of them might be lying as he is lying now but for his self-sacrifice. Don't tell me it is God's will! If I could believe it, I would wish I were a heathen, and worshipped a god of wood and stone!"

The Rector could only gaze in pained astonishment. Such an outburst was so unlike his usually calm and gentle sister. He judged she was beside herself with grief. She stood with clasped hands, wide-open eyes, unseeing, yet seeing, gazing beyond the confines of that room, catching a momentary vision of that light which 'never was, on land or sea.'

She became calm again--serenely calm.

"I see it," she said. "I understand. This is *not* God's will. It is not *His* work. His compassions fail not. His love is over all His children. With Him is the Fountain of Life. Does He not say, 'I will redeem them from death'? He will save this dear child from the grave. Leave me, please. I want to be alone--alone with Carol and God. I want to realize it. Yes; *God's will be done.* Life, not death, is God's will. I see it, I see so clearly."

To her husband she said softly, "I will ring if I want anything, dear. Don't let anyone come into the room until I ring."

When all had left the room, and the door was closed, she knelt beside the bed, with outstretched arms. It was a mother's cry to God for the life of a child that was as dear to her as her own. Hour after hour passed, and still she knelt. Words failed her, petition ceased: the realization came to her that God is Life: in Him we live, and move, and have our being. In Infinite Life there is no death. Death never is, and never can be God's will. The knowledge, the understanding of God as All-in-all vanquishes death! "O, death, I will be thy plagues. O, grave, I will be thy destruction!" (Hosea XIII., 14.)

The morning dawned, the bright sunbeams stole into the room. The boy opened his eyes. "Auntie,"--she was bending over him--"I have been dreaming. I thought I was in a field, and a bull tossed me high up into the air. But I knew in my dream, 'underneath are the everlasting arms.' Then I dreamed again, and two men were turning me about, and moving my arms and legs, and one said, 'There is not a broken bone, nor even a dislocation. It's a miracle.' I tried to say 'underneath are the everlasting arms,' but I could not speak."

The words were very faint and low. She bent close to catch them, then stopped them with a kiss, a pæan of joy in her heart. He spoke again: "Auntie, something is hurting me very much. I can't move."

"Do not try, darling, lie quite still. I will sit beside you and hold your hand."

A spasm of pain passed over his face, and he fell again into unconsciousness. But she had no fear, she knew that death had been vanquished by the knowledge that had come to her of life.

A low knock came to the door. She opened it, and found her maid there with a cup of tea. She took it from her saying: "Tell them all he lives, and he will live. But I wish to be alone with him for the present. No one is to trouble about me, I am quite well."

So she sat down again beside him, waiting and patiently watching, knowing that he would awake again to consciousness. It was nearly noon when he opened his eyes and spoke again. His voice was stronger:

"Auntie, was it a waking dream? Was I really in a field, and a bull tossed me? I am so aching all over me."

"Yes, darling."

"I think I remember now, Auntie. Rosebud and Estelle and Sylvia were there, and Jane called to me, 'Run, run!' They were not hurt, were they?"

"No, darling, not one of them."

"I am glad. Error is telling me I cannot move my legs and arms, Auntie. But it is not true. God's child cannot be bound like that. Does Cousin Alicia know?"

"I am sorry, Carol. I fear no one has thought to send her word."

"Will you send word now, Auntie--something quicker than a letter?"

"A telegram, dear?"

"Yes, Auntie, and put in, 'Please help Carol'."

"I will ask Uncle to send the message at once, dear."

When she opened the bedroom door, she found Colonel Mandeville pacing the corridor without. As a sentinel he had kept watch there throughout the night and a great part of the morning. He came into the room, and stood with one arm around his wife, looking down at Carol.

"Well, little man, so we are going to cheat the doctors?"

Carol didn't at all know what 'cheat' meant.

"Carol wishes you to let Miss Desmond know, dear. Will you wire at once? And say in the message, 'Please help Carol.' She will know what he means."

"I will gladly do so. Dr. Burton is downstairs, Emmeline. He had better come up now."

An expression of distress came over Carol's face.

"Auntie," he said, "don't let the doctor do anything to me, please."

"No one shall touch you, dear. But I should like Dr. Burton just to see you. He will tell me what I may give you to eat."

"I don't want anything, Auntie, only something to drink."

"Well, dear, he will tell me what will be best for you to have."

"I would like only water, please."

"You shall have some, dear, at once, and after that something else, I hope."

Dr. Burton came to the room, felt the patient's pulse, took his temperature, and looked at his tongue, but mercifully refrained from turning him about, to examine the bruises.

"I will send some medicine at once," he said to Mrs. Mandeville. "Give him a dose every hour. He has a very high temperature."

Downstairs he told Colonel Mandeville: "He may pull through if meningitis does not supervene."

But he left the house holding a very strong belief that meningitis would supervene. Not even the medicine, which was to be given every hour, could prevent it.

CHAPTER XIII.--THE RECTOR'S REFUSAL.

Mrs. Mandeville remained with Carol throughout the day, suffering no one to relieve her for one hour. As soon as he was told the telegram had been sent to Miss Desmond, he rested quite satisfied. But as the day wore on to evening, Mrs. Mandeville, standing over him, saw he was suffering acutely.

"You are in pain, darling," she said.

"Auntie, please don't ask me. I am trying to deny it. Couldn't you deny it for me, too?"

His lips were quivering; tears he strove bravely to keep back were stealing down his cheeks. How could she deny it? She would have given anything to be able to do so.

"Cousin Alicia must have had the telegram by this, Auntie, mustn't she?"

"Yes, dear; I think so. Being Sunday, it has taken longer to get through. Uncle has heard from the postmaster at W--, the nearest town, as the village telegraph office would be closed. The message has been sent on by messenger on horseback. So I think Miss Desmond must have received it by this time."

"She might have been out when it arrived, Auntie."

"Do you expect to feel less pain, dear, when Miss Desmond receives the telegram?"

"Yes, Auntie, I know I shall."

Seven o'clock--eight o'clock--nine o'clock passed. No reply telegram came. Mrs. Mandeville wrote a letter to go by the evening post, giving more details, and describing Carol's great desire to have a message from her. Dr. Burton came again at night. His instructions had been carried out. The medicine sent had been given every hour. Still the patient's temperature was higher, the pain he was suffering more acute, and the symptoms which pointed to meningitis more pronounced. "If he could sleep--a long natural sleep might save him," Dr. Burton said.

During the night Mrs. Mandeville was persuaded to take a little rest on a couch in the room, whilst Nurse and Colonel Mandeville kept watch beside the bed. Carol offered no opposition to anything that was done for him, and drank the medicine without a murmur, when the spoon was put to his lips.

In the morning, when Mrs. Mandeville was again alone with him, he said, "Auntie, I wonder why it hurts me to try to think. I tried so hard to go to sleep in the night and I could not. Then I began to think about Jesus when he was a little boy. We are not told that he was ever ill, and had to lie in bed, are we? But I felt quite sure, if he ever did, he would do just what his mother wanted him to do, wouldn't he? I know medicine and the bandages are not doing me any good, but it makes you happy for me to have them, doesn't it, Auntie?"

"Yes, darling; it seems all that we can do for you."

"If you understood Science, you could help me now, Auntie."

"Indeed then, I wish that I did, Carol."

"Sometimes the room seems to go dark, Auntie. In the night, two or three times, it was just as if the lamp went out, then lighted up again." Mrs. Mandeville understood enough to know this was very grave.

"Darling, will you try to lie quite still, and close your eyes--try not to think about anything?"

"Yes, Auntie, but I do hope a message will come from Cousin Alicia to-day. You will tell me when it comes, won't you?"

"Instantly, dear."

"I wish I could go to sleep, Auntie."

"I wish so too, my poor, dear boy."

"Could you move me a tiny bit, Auntie? I ache so lying in the same position. It seems so strange not to be able to move myself at all. Error seems very real."

Gently and lovingly, she tried to ease his position, but the least touch brought an expression of acute pain. She had to desist.

The long weary hours of that day passed, but no message, either a telegram or letter, came from Miss Desmond. Another wire was sent, asking for a reply. Still none came. Then, later on in the evening, a message was sent addressed to the housekeeper at Willmar Court, which quickly brought a reply: "Miss Desmond away. Impossible to forward messages."

Mrs. Mandeville told Carol very gently. He did not speak for some time, and, though he lay with closed eyes, she knew he was not sleeping.

Then he looked up at her:

"Auntie, when Jesus was in the boat, and the winds arose, and the waves surged high around the little boat, Jesus didn't command them at once to be still. The disciples had to awake him, and he rebuked them for their little faith. Shouldn't they have waited patiently, knowing it was all right? Sometimes it seems error has bound me with ropes, and I cannot move; sometimes it seems like waves washing over me. But I know that Love is saying to error's angry waves, 'Thus far, and no farther.' And just at the right moment the command will come: '*Peace, be still*.'"

Mrs. Mandeville hid her face in the pillow beside him, that he might not see the tears streaming from her eyes. She had lost again the faith which for a time had uplifted her to a realization of God's power to save the boy from death. In imagination she saw a new little grave in the churchyard with that word "Peace" graven in the marble headstone. She had been anxious for news from Miss Desmond because Carol wished it so much. She had little hope or faith that injuries, such as his, could in any way be alleviated by Miss Desmond's knowledge of Christian Science. The night passed again, and not for one hour did sleep close the suffering boy's eyes. He had been unconscious for a time, murmuring incoherently; but it was not sleep.

Dr. Burton said very little when he came in the morning; he only looked graver and sadder. By telegram he had been in constant communication with Sir Wilfrid Wynne, and he knew that, humanly speaking, nothing more could be done for the boy than was being done. Yet there was no progress.

"How I wish there was something I could do for you, Carol!" Mrs. Mandeville said, as she sat beside him.

"Auntie, there is something, if Uncle Raymond will let you have it. I know I should fall asleep if you read *Science and Health* to me. I always used to when I was ill before, and Cousin Alicia read it to me, even before I began to understand it."

"I will go to the rectory at once, dear, and ask Uncle for the book. Promise me to lie with closed eyes; and try not even to think about anything whilst I am away."

She would not write, nor send a message, fearing a refusal. As soon as Nurse came to take her place she left the room, and the house. There was a path through the park direct to the rectory. It was less than ten minutes' walk.

The Rector looked up in astonishment as his sister, hatless and coatless (it was a chilly September day), entered the room. "What is it, Emmeline? Is Carol worse?" he asked. Her flushed, distressed face suggested the question.

"I do not know if he is worse. He is just as ill as he can be, and is suffering cruelly. I want you to let me have that book you took from him, Raymond, *Science and Health*. He thinks if I read it to him he will fall asleep. He has not

- 47 -

slept yet, and this is the third day since the accident." The Rector's face, which before had been grave and kindly, now grew stern and resolute. "I am sorry, Emmeline, but I cannot let you have it. That book will never pass from my hands to his as long as I am his guardian. He knows too much already of its pernicious doctrines. Better better--anything than that his faith in its teachings should be strengthened."

"Do you mean better that he should die, Raymond?"

"Yes, Emmeline, better that--even that."

"Oh, Raymond, how can you hold such a thought? I do not know what the book is nor what it teaches. But I do know what is the fruit of it; and who was it said, 'A tree is known by its fruit; a corrupt tree cannot bring forth good fruit'?"

"We need not discuss that, Emmeline. We both know whose words those are. Still, I maintain that the teachings of that book, being pernicious, cannot bring forth good fruit."

"But, Raymond, is not gentleness, faith and love--such as Carol's--good fruit? Jesus to him did not live two thousand years ago. He is living to-day. He is looking to him, as the disciples looked, when the storm arose at sea. His love and his faith are beautiful to witness. I have always tried to teach my children the love of God, but Carol possesses something I have not been able to give them, because I do not possess it myself. I think it is understanding. He seems to understand the Bible much better than I do."

"I am sorry to hear you speak like this, Emmeline. In any difficulty why do you not come to me? Surely there are books enough here to explain, or to throw a light on anything that is not clear to you."

The Rector looked round at his well-filled book-shelves: old books and new books; works of the early Fathers and the latest theological treatise.

"I cannot explain what it is I want, Raymond. I only know I always seem to be groping after something, and I cannot find it. But when I am talking to Carol, I seem nearer to it. Raymond, won't you let me have that book--just for to-day--I will return it to you to-morrow?"

"No, Emmeline. Not for one hour."

"You are cruel, Raymond, when the boy is suffering so, and it is all he asks you. If there were a shop near where I could buy a copy, I would straightway do so. I will know for myself what the book teaches. I shall write to Miss Desmond, and ask her to get me a copy."

"Of course, Emmeline, if you choose to do that, I have no control over your actions. I have over Carol's, and I shall exercise it."

Then Mrs. Mandeville broke down and burst into tears. "Perhaps you won't have power long. Oh, Raymond! You do not realize how ill he is! If meningitis sets in, Dr. Burton says it will be a matter of only a few hours. If I were asking for a Buddhist or a Mohammedan book, it would be right for you to let me have it."

"No, my dear sister. I am not a believer in the doctrine that the end justifies the means. I will pray for Carol, and for you too. I am sorry to see you so overwrought."

"Then you absolutely refuse, Raymond?"

"I do, Emmeline--absolutely."

Without a word Mrs. Mandeville turned and left the room.

CHAPTER XIV.
"HE GIVETH HIS BELOVED SLEEP."

Softly and lightly as Mrs. Mandeville re-entered Carol's room, he heard her. He had been listening for her footsteps, whilst obedient to her desire, lying with closed eyelids.

She was spared the pain of telling him she had been unsuccessful. He read it in her face.

"Auntie, dear, please don't look so troubled. Uncle Raymond does not understand. It is quite all right. Love can always find a way." Mrs. Mandeville almost smiled through her unshed tears. How great was her love for the boy, yet she could think of no way by which what he wanted could be immediately procured. Even she did not fully realize how he was waiting and yearning for that healing touch, which comes

'More softly than the dew is shed

Or cloud is floated overhead.'

Nurse left the room, and Mrs. Mandeville again took her place by the bedside.

In less than an hour a maid came to the bedroom door, asking in a whisper, "Can I speak to you a moment, ma'am?"

"What is it, Withers?" Mrs. Mandeville asked.

"A Mr. Higgs from the village is downstairs. He came to inquire after Master Carol. He said he would like the young gentleman to know he has walked from the village to the Manor."

The words were spoken at the door very softly, but Carol heard.

"Oh, Auntie, I am glad!" he said. "Could Mr. Higgs come here? I should like to speak to him."

"Darling, I am afraid it will excite you to see him. The doctor's orders are that you are to be kept perfectly quiet."

"It won't excite me, Auntie; and what makes me very happy cannot hurt me."

"You may bring Mr. Higgs to see Master Carol since he wishes it so much, Withers."

No one but those who were nursing him had been admitted to the room. The maid was surprised as she took the message, and then brought the old man to the room.

"God bless 'ee, Master Carol, God bless 'ee. Aye, I don't know how to say it often enough, when I think it's all along o' the blessed truth you taught me I'm free of the rheumatiz. I met Farmer Stubbins on my way, and he says, 'Why, Higgs, you're walking along quite spry. What's become o' your rheumatiz?' 'Gone, thank the Lord,' says I, 'never to return.' 'Oh! and what may you have done to get rid of it?' he asks, being crippled himself with the same. 'I ain't done nothing,' I replied. Then I says, 'Farmer Stubbins, you and me was boys together, and we sang in the village choir. Do you mind there's a verse in the Psalms--aye, we've sung it many a time; but we just didn't think o' the words--it was the music we thought about. "He sent His word and healed them." That's just what the Lord has done. He has sent His word and healed me, and He sent it by the mouth of one of His dear children.'"

Carol's face was radiant with joy. Anxiously watching him, Mrs. Mandeville could not fear that the old man's talk could harm him.

Then, after fumbling in his coat pocket, he drew forth a little book carefully folded in soft paper.

"I've got it, Master Carol. It came this morning--the little book you've told me about. My daughter wrote for me. We didn't quite know where to write, so we just addressed the letter: 'Christian Science Church, London,' and a kind lady has sent me this book. It isn't quite new, and she writes that I shall value it more if it costs me something. I am just to pay what I can, and send the money as I am able."

He was unfolding the paper covering as he spoke, and then held out a small copy of *Science and Health*.

"Oh, Auntie, isn't Love beautiful! You see Love *has* found a way. Mr. Higgs will lend it to you to read to me a little time--won't you, Mr. Higgs?"

"I'll be very happy to, Master Carol."

Mrs. Mandeville took the book with almost a feeling of awe. It had come so wonderfully, yet so simply. She thought of the words: "He sent His angel."

She pointed to a chair, saying, "Please be seated, Mr. Higgs, whilst I read. Is there any particular part you would like me to read, Carol?" she asked, turning over the pages.

"No, Auntie--just open the book; let Love find the place."

"Carol, you so frequently speak of Love as of a personality. What do you mean, dear?"

"Auntie, God is Love. But when we speak of God, it seems we must bow our head, and think reverently of the great 'I Am.' But when we speak of Love--we can just creep into Love's arms, and ask Love anything."

"Even to find a place in a book," Mrs. Mandeville said with a smile.

"Yes, Auntie--even that."

Then she opened the book. It opened at page 494, and the first sentence she read was: "Divine Love always has met and always will meet every human need."

A smile rested on the boy's face, his sufferings were forgotten, as the dear familiar words fell on his ear. Love had not failed him.

Mrs. Mandeville never knew afterwards how long she read. She became entranced, absorbed.

When she turned to look at him, he was asleep. She quietly rose, and with one whispered word asked Mr. Higgs to follow her.

Withers was still waiting without.

"Take Mr. Higgs to the housekeeper's room, Withers, and ask her to give him a substantial tea. Then send word to the stables--when he is ready--I wish Parker to drive him to his home in my basket chaise. It is only a step from the ground. You will easily get in and out. I am deeply indebted to you for coming this afternoon, Mr. Higgs. My dear boy needed sleep so much. It was vitally necessary for him. He was so sure he would sleep, if I could read *Science and Health* to him, and I did not know how to procure a copy of the book."

"May I leave this with you, ma'am?"

"If you will be so kind for a day or two."

"Isn't Love beautiful!" the old man said to himself, repeating Carol's words, as he followed the maid to the housekeeper's room.

CHAPTER XV.--LETTERS AND TELEGRAMS REACH COUSIN ALICIA.

Carol's sleep lasted two hours. Then he awoke, with something of his old bright smile. Mrs. Mandeville was still watching beside him.

"Auntie, I have been asleep."

"Yes, darling, I know. I have been watching you. It was a beautiful sleep. I thought as I sat beside you of the words, 'He giveth His beloved sleep.' I am sure you are better for it."

"Yes, Auntie, it was lovely, and my back doesn't hurt me quite so much. But I cannot move my legs yet."

"Do not try, dear."

"Did I dream it, Auntie, or were you reading *Science and Health* to me?"

"It was not a dream, dear. Mr. Higgs came and brought the book, and he has left it with me."

"I remember now, Auntie. Was it not nice of him to come? Has any message come yet from Cousin Alicia?"

"No, love; I cannot understand why the letters and telegrams are not forwarded to her."

"There is some reason, I know, Auntie. We shall understand by and by." She gave him some soda and milk, which was all the doctor would let him have.

"I should like to see Rosebud, Auntie. Couldn't she come for a little while?"

Mrs. Mandeville had already admitted one visitor against orders. Dare she act on her own responsibility a second time? She began to realize how much the doctor's fears of developments, which might or might not follow, were influencing her, though, happily, she was not able to influence Carol. He had no fear.

"I think it must be almost Rosebud's bedtime, dear; but she shall come for a few minutes."

After sending a message to the nursery for Rosebud, her eye fell on the medicine bottle. "Oh, Carol, I didn't give you your medicine this afternoon. It was just time for it when Mr. Higgs came, and afterwards you were asleep. It is time again for it now. I see it must be fresh medicine; it is a different color."

"Auntie, Mr. Higgs was my doctor, this afternoon. The medicine he brought sent me to sleep, and I do not ache quite so much. Must I take this drug medicine as well?"

Mrs. Mandeville had poured out a dose, and now held the glass in her hand.

"You are right, Carol. I can see a decided improvement. I will not ask you to drink this."

She emptied the contents of the glass away. A few minutes afterwards Rosebud's sweet voice was piping at the door:

"Me's 'tome to see Tarol."

Mrs. Mandeville lifted her up to kiss Carol, very carefully guarding her from touching him anywhere.

"You must only kiss Carol, darling." The little arms were about to twine themselves around him. "Me does 'ove 'ou, Tarol, so welly much."

The boy would have liked to hold her closely to him, but he could not raise an arm.

"It does make me so happy to see Rosebud again, Auntie. Perhaps to-morrow I shall be able to see all my cousins."

Mrs. Mandeville did not say, but she thought it would be many "to-morrows" before he would be strong enough to receive them all in his room.

"Now run back to the nursery, darling," she said to the wee girlie.

"Take a good-night kiss to Sylvia and Estelle, will you Rosebud?" Carol said. Then she had to be lifted up again to receive a kiss for "eberybody."

Mrs. Mandeville sat silent by the bedside for some time after Rosebud left the room. Then she said in a very low, soft voice, "Do you remember, Carol, coming to my room one day when I lay prostrate with one of my bad headaches?"

"Yes, Auntie; I remember quite well."

"I was very ungrateful, Carol, I would not let myself acknowledge it was your little prayer that took it away. Yet I knew it was, for I had never lost a headache like that before."

"Yes, Auntie, I knew Christian Science had helped you. But I thought you did not understand."

She kissed him very tenderly. "I am not ungrateful any longer, dear. I acknowledge the debt. Now I must not let you talk any more or Dr. Burton will insist upon having a trained nurse. He has suggested it several times."

"He couldn't keep you away from me, could he, Auntie?"

"I think he would find it a trifle difficult, dear."

"But I want you to go downstairs to dinner to-night, Auntie. Uncle will like to have you, and Nurse will stay with me."

"Perhaps I will go then, for an hour, dear."

So, later on, to everyone's surprise Mrs. Mandeville appeared at the dinner table, and was so bright they all knew, without asking, that Carol was improving, though he had not been pronounced out of danger.

Nurse was quietly making all the needful little preparations for the night when Carol asked her to place the clock where he could see it as he lay in bed.

"The nights seem so long when I cannot sleep, Nurse. I like to watch the fingers of the clock, then I know how long it will be before the light can peep through the curtains."

Nurse found a position where he could see it quite well, even though he could not raise his head from the pillows. Then, standing over him, she said: "Dearie, you are in pain. Couldn't I ease your position just a little?"

"No, Nurse, please don't touch me, the bruises seem so real. I ought to be able to deny them, and I cannot."

"And would it make them better to deny them, Master Carol?"

"Oh, yes, Nurse. You are thinking the bruises are very sore and painful, are you not?"

Yes, Nurse was decidedly dwelling in thought upon the pain the boy must be suffering from such a bruised condition.

"If you could think, Nurse, that there is no sensation in matter, that the pain is all in mind: in my mind and your mind, and Auntie's and the doctor's. You are all thinking how I must be suffering. If only someone would help me to deny it!"

"I wish I could, Master Carol."

But it was double Dutch to Nurse to try to understand that the pain was in mind, and not in the poor bruised body.

It was half-past nine when she moved the time-piece so that Carol could see it, and he at once began to count how many hours it would be till morning. At ten o'clock Mrs. Mandeville returned to the room, followed by Dr. Burton. Nurse held up a warning finger as they entered: the boy was asleep.

"This is splendid! How long has he slept?" the doctor asked.

"It was just after half-past nine, sir. He seemed in great pain, I thought there was no hope of sleep for him, and all at once he just dropped off without a word."

It was such a beautiful sleep, calm, peaceful, untroubled by fret or moan. Mrs. Mandeville and the doctor watched beside him an hour; then the doctor left, and Mrs. Mandeville was persuaded to go to her own room for a night's rest, leaving Nurse in charge. They did not know, nor could they have understood had they known, how, far away, a woman, 'clad in the whole armour of God,' was fighting for him: fighting error with 'the sword of the Spirit.'

Letters and telegrams had at last reached Cousin Alicia.

CHAPTER XVI.--"IT IS A MIRACLE."

The next morning about eight o'clock, Nurse came to Mrs. Mandeville's room, an expression of amazement, almost of consternation, on her face.

"What is it, Nurse? Is Master Carol worse?" Mrs. Mandeville asked in alarm.

"No, ma'am; I cannot say he is worse. He says he is well, and wants to get up for breakfast. He slept all through the night, just as you left him, and never wakened till half-past seven this morning. He is certainly not feverish or delirious, but he talks so strangely. He says error has all gone, and he is free. I had quite a difficulty to prevent him from getting out of bed to come to you. I have sent a messenger for Dr. Burton."

"That is right, Nurse. Go back to him. I will come at once." Mrs. Mandeville was not long slipping into a morning wrap, and following Nurse to Carol's room.

As soon as she reached the bedside, he sprang up, and held her in a close embrace, both arms round her neck. "Auntie, Auntie, isn't it beautiful? I am free! Error has quite gone. I know Cousin Alicia has had the telegrams now. You can rub your hand down my back. It does not hurt me now, nor the bruises."

"Carol, dear, I cannot understand it. It seems so wonderful. I am afraid you ought not to be sitting up like this."

"Oh, Auntie, there is nothing to be afraid about. Error cast out cannot come back again. I am so hungry. I do want to get up to breakfast."

"Darling, you must lie still until Dr. Burton has seen you. I could not consent for you to get up yet. It does indeed seem beautiful for you to be so much better, I cannot realize it, and I cannot understand, Carol, why Miss Desmond's prayers for you should be so quickly answered, when I am sure I love you just as dearly. I prayed for you, and Uncle Raymond prayed, yet--yet I cannot feel that our prayers helped you."

She had tenderly laid him back upon the pillow. She could not get rid of the fear that it was not good for him to be using his back.

He was silent a few minutes, the old thoughtful expression on his face which she knew so well. Then he said:

"Auntie, the sun was shining this morning long before Nurse drew aside the curtains, and let the light into my room. Suppose while the curtain was drawn I had kept saying, 'Please, dear sun, do shine into my room, and send the darkness away.' It would have had no effect. It would have been foolish, wouldn't it? Well, Auntie, the light of Truth, like the sunlight is everywhere, but we can shut it out of our consciousness by a curtain of false beliefs. Cousin Alicia has not asked God to make me better. She has just known that God's child is always perfect. As Nurse drew aside the curtain to let in the sunlight, she has drawn aside the curtain of false beliefs that were around me, and then Truth came and healed me. Jesus said 'the Truth shall make you free.' It is just as true, Auntie, as if he had said, 'When light appears, darkness disappears.' Wherever Truth appears, error shall flee away, because it is not from God. It is the opposite of God's law. I love that beautiful verse of the hymn more than I have ever loved it, because I can say again:

'The healing of the seamless dress

Is by our beds of pain.'

Christ is Truth, and Truth is the Christ. I was asleep when he came to me. But just as Jesus spoke to the angry waves the Christ has commanded error, 'Peace, be still.' Oh, Auntie! cannot you believe I am quite well? 'I am the Father's perfect child. I have the gift from God, dominion over all.'"

She was longing to realize that it was as the boy said, and she had nothing to fear. Yet it was difficult.

Dr. Burton was out when the messenger from the Manor went for him. He had not returned from a night case to which he had been summoned. Mrs. Burton promised that he would go immediately on his return. Shortly after ten o'clock Dr. Burton arrived, expecting to find from the urgent message that had reached him a change for the worse in his patient. He was considerably taken aback as he entered the room to hear a ripple of laughter, and the boy with a radiant face, sitting upright in bed, who, the day before, had not been able to raise his head from the pillow.

"What does this mean?" Dr. Burton asked in a tone of voice in which surprise became almost consternation.

"I cannot tell you anything, Doctor, except that Carol slept all night and woke this morning feeling quite well and hungry. He has had a fairly substantial breakfast," Mrs. Mandeville said. The doctor then thoroughly examined him, felt his pulse, took his temperature, and when he looked on the places where the terrible bruises had been, and saw only a faint discoloration, he said:

"It is a miracle!"

"No, Doctor," said Carol, quietly, "it is Christian Science."

"Then what is Christian Science?" the doctor asked.

But the boy was silent. He could talk to his aunt on the subject, but not to the doctor.

At that moment a maid brought a telegram to Mrs. Mandeville. It was from Miss Desmond. She read it, and passed it on to Dr. Burton. It was brief: "Letters and telegrams reached me 9.30 last evening. Regret unavoidable delay. Kindly wire if all is well. Letter to Carol follows." The doctor and Mrs. Mandeville simply looked at each other in speechless wonderment, one thought engrossing them. It was shortly after 9.30 the night before that Carol fell into the sleep from which he had awakened well.

"It is at last a message from Cousin Alicia," Mrs. Mandeville then said to Carol. "Our letters and telegrams did not reach her till 9.30 last evening."

"Yes, Auntie, I knew it, and I know she has worked for me all night."

Both Mrs. Mandeville and the doctor would have liked to understand what the boy meant by that one word "worked." But neither questioned him then.

"I can get up now, Doctor, cannot I?" Carol asked.

"Yes, there is no reason that I can see for keeping you in bed. All the same," turning to Mrs. Mandeville, "I should say he may as well be kept fairly quiet for a day or two--not commence running races, or any other juvenile sports."

"You can trust me, Doctor," Mrs. Mandeville remarked, smiling.

"It seems to me you should consult the lady who has worked for him all night with such marvellous success. I can scarcely consider him my patient now."

"Doctor, I thank you very much for all you tried to do for me. You were very kind and gentle to me."

"Tut-tut, boy! Why, that's of course."

All the same the doctor was pleased with the boy's simple recognition of his services. He would indeed have done more, had he been able. He walked home slowly and thoughtfully, pondering that question, which he had asked the boy, thinking of a lecture which he had given a few weeks before in a crowded parish room; how he himself had answered the question--What is Christian Science?--to the convulsive amusement of his audience. He had dipped into a book--the text-book of Christian Science--made copious extracts and so satisfied himself that he understood the subject sufficiently to be able to warn people against the teachings of Christian Science.

Mrs. Burton was watching for his return. She was anxious for news of the boy, fearing the early message which had been sent for the doctor must mean that he was worse. By her side, in the garden, seated in a little wheelchair, was her only child, a girl of ten, who after a fall downstairs when she was five years old, causing an injury to her spine, had lost the use of her legs. There seemed no hope of her ever being able to walk again, since all the doctors who had seen her had not been able to do anything for her.

"How is the boy?" asked Mrs. Burton, as the doctor entered the garden in front of the house.

"He is well," was the brief reply.

"You don't mean?--" Mrs. Burton began in an alarmed tone.

"I mean exactly what I say--the boy is well."

"But, dear, how can that be, when he was so ill yesterday?"

"I cannot tell you. He says it is Christian Science. I say it is a miracle."

"Father, he won't lose the use of his legs, will he?" the little girl asked.

"No, Eloise, I think there will be no such effects from the fall, as unhappily there were in your case."

"I am glad, Father, he is such a nice, kind boy!"

The child had grieved, fearing that he might be crippled like herself.

"Christian Science must be different from what you described at the lecture, dear. Do you think I might go and see Carol? I should like to hear from him what it is that has made him well so quickly. I owe Mrs. Mandeville a call."

"Go and pay it, then. Perhaps the boy will talk to you. He did not seem to care to answer my questions."

The doctor passed into the house with the thought that he would borrow that book again, and see if he could get a better understanding of the subject himself.

CHAPTER XVII.--MRS. BURTON VISITS CAROL.

Shortly after the doctor left Carol's room, the maid entered to say the Rector was downstairs. Could he come up?

"I will speak with the Rector before he comes upstairs," Mrs. Mandeville said, and left the room for that purpose.

The news had reached the Rector that Dr. Burton had been sent for early that morning, and he also surmised that the boy must be worse. But the servants had assured him that such was not the case before Mrs. Mandeville joined him in the library.

"What is this I hear about Carol, Emmeline? He is not worse, yet you sent for Dr. Burton before breakfast. I felt quite alarmed."

"We could not understand it, Raymond. I must confess to feeling afraid it was not true. Carol is quite well. Dr. Burton admits it. He says it is a miracle. Carol says it is Christian Science. Dear Raymond, I want to beg you before you see Carol not to say anything to shake his faith. It is so beautiful."

"His faith in what? In that heresy called Christian Science, which is neither Science nor Christian?"

"Oh, Raymond, I cannot help thinking you are mistaken in your judgment. I do not, as I told you before, quite understand what Christian Science is, but this I know, I have never met a character so Christ-like as Carol's. All day yesterday he lay in such pain from those terrible bruises, and the injury to his spine and head, that we could not move him in the effort to ease his position without increasing the pain. To-day it is all gone. What has taken it away? He says the Christ--Truth has come to him and healed him. If we believe Jesus' words: 'Lo, I am with you always even to the end of the world'--why should it not be true? Cannot the spiritual Christ say as Jesus so often said, 'According to your faith be it unto you'?"

"Of course! But that is not Christian Science."

"Yes, Raymond, that is what Carol seems to have learned from Christian Science. Heaven to him is not a far-off locality, it is here--all around him, and God is ever-present Love. His one thought--his one desire seems to be to possess that Mind which was also in Christ Jesus. What can you say against such teaching?"

The Rector had evidently nothing to say. He remarked briefly, "If I may, I will go up and see the boy now. I am pressed for time."

"Yes, Raymond, he will be pleased to see you."

She let him go alone, and did not afterwards inquire what had passed between the boy and his uncle.

Later in the day Mrs. Mandeville took Percy to Carol's room. The boy had begged so frequently to be allowed to see his cousin. "Just to tell him I am sorry," he said.

Carol had forgotten all about it.

"Sorry for what, dear Percy?" he inquired, when Percy, in faltering accents, asked to be forgiven.

"Oh, I think I remember now, Percy, you said something that was not quite kind, but I knew at the time that you did not mean it. So why should we remember any more about it?"

"You are just the bravest fellow I know, Carol. I have told all the boys at school how you stood and faced the bull. They think a tremendous lot of you for it. So it won't matter when you come with us if you can't play football or cricket. You will be the hero of the school."

Then Mrs. Mandeville left the boys together for a little while. Percy was only too delighted to be able to tell Carol of all that was happening at school, the matches that had been played, and those that were to come off shortly.

When Mrs. Burton called that same afternoon, she expressed her great desire to see and talk with Carol. Mrs. Mandeville readily assented, remarking that she felt sure Carol would be delighted to see her. As there were other visitors present, she was not able to accompany her herself. A maid therefore conducted her to Carol's room. Nurse was sitting with him. As Mrs. Burton intimated that she had come to have a little talk with Master Carol, she left the room.

"Eloise sends her love to you, dear Carol. She is so happy to know you are so wonderfully better. We feared so much that you, too, might be crippled for life, as she has been, by a fall. The spinal concussion caused her to lose the use of her legs. We have consulted the first specialists, but they have never been able to do anything for her. When the doctor told me this morning how miraculously you have been healed, I felt I must come and ask you to tell me something about it. Tell me, dear Carol, what is Christian Science?"

The boy looked up, but not at Mrs. Burton. That far-away dreamy look came to his eyes, which his cousins knew so well. It was such a big question to try to answer. It seemed minutes before he spoke. Then he said: "I think

Christian Science means knowledge--a knowledge of God; and as we gain this knowledge we draw nearer to Him. Cousin Alicia used to tell me we are all God's children, but we have wandered so far away from Him. We are prodigals, dwelling in that far country where we are fed, like the swine, on husks. Christian Science just teaches us the way back to our Father's house; and as we find the road and walk in it, we lose the evils that tormented us. Jesus was our elder brother who never left his Father's house. Although he lived on earth, it was still his Father's house, because he lived always in the consciousness of good. And that is what we have to try to do. It seemed easier when I was with Cousin Alicia."

There was just a note of sadness and regret in the boy's voice.

"What a beautiful thought, Carol, 'living in the consciousness of good.' But, dear, how can we do it, with sickness, sorrow, and sin, all around? When I look at my wee girlie, I can never know joy or happiness; her young life to be so cruelly blighted through the carelessness of a maid. Every child I see running about free and happy is like a dagger in my heart, as I know that she should be the same."

"When Cousin Alicia came from America after my mother's death, I was very ill, and the doctors said I could never be better. But she knew that I could. She said, 'You are God's child, dear Carol, and all God's children are spiritual, and therefore perfect. Awake from this dream of suffering and pain.' Every day she used to talk to me, until she led me to understand what it is to live in the consciousness of good, and then I was well."

"Oh, Carol, it seems too wonderful to be true! Do you think that something might be done for my little girl?"

"Why, of course. I am sure if you will take her to my home, Cousin Alicia will teach her as she taught me. She is always so happy to teach people about Christian Science. Shall I write and tell her you will take Eloise to her?"

"Thank you, dear Carol, but I think, perhaps, before you write, I must ask Dr. Burton. If he is willing, I will gladly take my little girl to Miss Desmond."

Mrs. Burton did not stay much longer. On leaving, she tenderly kissed Carol. "Dear boy, you have given me hope. You cannot think what it has been to a mother's heart to be so long hopeless," she said.

The little crippled Eloise was watching from her nursery window for her mother's return. Mrs. Burton went straight to her.

"Have you seen Carol, Mother?" she asked.

"Yes, darling, and I have had such a sweet talk with him. He has made me so happy. I seem to see you running about like other children."

"Oh, Mother, wouldn't that be lovely! And is he really well?"

"It seems so, dear. Mrs. Mandeville is keeping him quietly in his own room to-day. But he seemed so well and happy. He wants me to take you into Devonshire to stay with his cousin. He says she will teach us what she has taught him--and then--Oh, Eloise, my darling, you, too, would be well and strong, no longer a little crippled girl."

"What is it, Mother, that he has been taught?"

"It seems something so wonderful and beautiful, dear. He says that dwelling in the consciousness of good is dwelling in our Father's house, but, like the prodigal son in the parable, we have wandered away into that far country where all sorts of evils can befall us. My girlie, we will try to find our way together into this happy understanding of good which causes the fetters to fall. I will speak to Father to-night and ask him to let me take you."

"Do--*do*, please, Mother."

Mrs. Burton waited that evening until it was past the hour for patients to call at the surgery. Then she went to her husband's consulting-room.

The doctor was sitting at his desk, an open letter before him. His pen was in his hand, but he was not writing. The answer to the letter seemed to require much thought. It was only partly written.

"Are you very busy, dear?" Mrs. Burton said, softly twining one arm around his neck. She was almost nervous. It was a great request she was about to proffer. She did not quite know how it would be received.

"Not particularly, love, if you want anything. What is it?"

"I want to tell you I had a beautiful talk with Carol this afternoon, and he is so kind as to ask me to take Eloise to stay with his cousin at his home in Devonshire, that she--that she might teach us what she has taught him. You know, dear, we have done everything we can--there is no other hope for her."

"And you think there may be hope in this--Christian Science?"

"I feel sure of it--since I have seen Carol."

The doctor smiled. The humor of the situation struck him. He pointed to the open letter on his desk.

"That letter," he said, "is from the Vicar of B-- asking me to give in his Parish Room the lecture which I gave at B--."

"Oh!" There was an accent of pain in Mrs. Burton's voice. "You are not going to?"

"Why do you object? The lecture was well received, you remember."

"Yes, but even at the time when the people laughed and applauded, it seemed to hurt me. I couldn't help thinking if these people, who call themselves Christian Scientists, believe so absolutely in the Christ healing, it was what the early Christians believed, and practised, and they were persecuted. When Christ spoke to Saul of Tarsus, he did not say, 'Why persecutest thou my followers?' He said 'Why persecutest thou *me*?'

"So I felt that night that the laughter and ridicule of all in the room were as stones thrown not at people, but at the Christ. Don't tell me, dear, that you are going to give that lecture again."

"I am not. That boy's radiant face would come between me and any audience I might think to address. I have commenced a letter to the Vicar, telling him I feel I cannot lecture on the subject again."

"And I may take Eloise to Willmar Court?"

"You may. Should she regain the use of her legs, as a result of the visit, I will espouse the Cause I once derided. After witnessing Carol's marvellous recovery, it does not seem impossible."

CHAPTER XVIII.--HAPPY THOUGHTS.

After Mrs. Burton left Carol, Edith came and had tea with him, and after tea all his cousins were allowed to visit him for a little time. They could not understand how the sadness and gloom in the house had been dispelled. It was like the sun shining through clouds on a rainy day. He was so bright and happy, just their own dear Carol again. There was one subject of which he never spoke to his cousins; so they could not know why, the day before, the house was hushed, and he could not be seen because he was so ill, and to-day there seemed nothing at all the matter with him.

When Mrs. Mandeville went the round of the children's rooms after dinner, she found Carol waiting for her in the old way, just as if there had been no break, no agony of sorrow and suspense.

"I hoped to find you asleep, darling," she said. "Has it been too much excitement having so many in your room?"

"Oh, no, Auntie. I loved to see them all again. I have had such happy thoughts. Isn't it nice to be kept awake by happy thoughts? Happy thoughts are good thoughts, and good thoughts come from God. Shall I tell you, Auntie, dear, what I have been thinking about?"

"Wouldn't it be better to tell me in the morning, dearie? It is rather late for a little boy who was an invalid only yesterday to be kept awake even by happy thoughts."

"I would rather tell you to-night, Auntie. You do not quite understand, do you, that when error is cast out, it is done with, and we do not need to remember anything about it."

"Then tell me, love, what you have been thinking about."

"I began first of all, Auntie, thinking about Peter."

Mrs. Mandeville's thoughts at once went to the stables, where one of the horses was named Peter.

"Peter, dear?" Just a note of surprise in her voice.

"Yes, Auntie, when Jesus called Peter to come to him on the water, at first he was not afraid, and he got out of the boat to go to him. Then he began to be afraid, and as soon as fear crept in, he began to sink. Auntie, I was just like that. At first I was not afraid of the bull. I knew God had given me dominion, and I was trying to realize it. Then the moment I began to be afraid, the bull tossed me. As I was thinking of this perhaps I fell asleep, and it was a dream. But it was so real. I seemed to see Peter standing by the bed, but he didn't look like the picture in the stained-glass window, and he spoke so kindly and gently. 'Little brother,' he said, 'you have not learned to trust the Master yet.' It was just as if he remembered there was a time when his faith had failed. I wanted to ask him something, but he was not there, and I was quite wide awake. May it perhaps be, Auntie, that as Christ 'walks life's troubled angry sea,' they are with him, those disciples who were always with Jesus, especially Peter, and James, and John; and they are working now, doing his bidding, as they did it in Galilee, watching over and helping those who are still fighting?"

"It may be, Carol, we cannot tell. It seems that events which happened two thousand years ago are to you but as yesterday."

"Why, yes, Auntie; time in God's kingdom is not measured by years and weeks and months. I shall just love now to think about Peter, and know that my faith will grow stronger, as his did. There are many people who would not have been afraid of the bull. Cousin Alicia told me of a lady in India who, one day, came quite close to a cobra. But she was not afraid, and as she stood quite still and looked at it, the cobra coiled itself into a heap and went to sleep. Then she told me of a gentleman who was shooting game in Africa, and once he was in a position when he could not fire, and a leopard was only a few yards from him, but the animal did not attack him, it ran away into the desert. The lady and the gentleman knew and realized that they had dominion; I hope I shall understand it better some day, and not be afraid of anything."

"You have been taught some strange things, Carol, still they are beautiful; it seems almost too beautiful to be true."

"Oh, Auntie, nothing can be too beautiful to be true, because only good, and good is always beautiful, is real; evil, and evil is always ugly, is unreal."

"Carol, darling, I wish I could believe that. You are leading me in strange paths. I must not let you talk any more to-night. I am quite sure that it is time a little boy, who has lost so much sleep lately, tried to make up for it."

But as she bent over him to kiss him, he clung both arms around her neck, keeping her a willing captive for some minutes longer.

"Auntie, I am so longing for Cousin Alicia's letter," were his last words as she left the room.

CHAPTER XIX.--THE REASON OF THE DELAY.

The next morning Carol rose at his usual time, and breakfasted with his cousins in the school-room. Miss Markham looked at him with puzzled eyes, especially when he told her he was quite ready to begin lessons again. She could not understand it. There seemed to be some mystery connected with his marvellous recovery from what everybody believed to be serious injuries. She took the opportunity, when his cousins were out of the room, to ask him quietly, "What has made you well so quickly, Carol?"

"Ask Auntie, please, Miss Markham, I am not allowed to talk about it," he replied. Miss Markham's wonderment was considerably increased, for Mrs. Mandeville had only told her, when the boy first came to the Manor, that he had been taught religious tenets which were altogether unorthodox. She did not then connect that remark with the boy's quick recovery. He often made remarks which surprised her. Sometimes she pondered over a remark he had made, and found there was more in it than at first had appeared. If she attempted to draw him out by questions, he became strangely silent and reserved. Once, it was during a history lesson, Carol exclaimed, "But evil could have no power, Miss Markham, if everyone knew that God--good-- governs. If we had no belief in evil, evil could not hurt us."

Thinking over the words afterwards, Miss Markham admitted to herself that to acknowledge the omnipotence of God, must deprive evil of any power. But she wondered how it was Carol had come to see it so clearly. She could not, however, draw him to talk any more on the subject. After breakfast Mrs. Mandeville came to the school-room with the longed-for letter in her hand, and, as permission was readily given, Carol went to his own room to read it. Eagerly he broke open the envelope, and read:

"WILLMAR COURT,

SOUTH DEVON.

"*My dear, dear Carol,*

"The telegram in answer to mine this morning has just arrived. I waited for it before commencing my letter to you. I rejoice for you, Truth has triumphed, error has fallen. When I returned to the Court last night, after being absent since Saturday afternoon, I found telegrams and letters awaiting me. On learning that the first telegram asking for help for you was more than three days old, I had to fight error on my own account, before I could fight it on yours. How quick error is to find the weak parts of our armor. My human love for you, darling, opened wide the portals, and a crowd of wrong thoughts rushed in. I found myself wondering why it should have so happened that I should be away, when I seemed most wanted, and under circumstances which made it impossible for the telegrams to be sent on.

"Then, in this sudden tempest of doubts and fears which had rushed upon me, came the words, calm, sweet, tender: 'I, if I, be lifted up, will draw all men unto me.' And I knew, I was absolutely sure, however great were the sense sufferings, Carol had held steadfastly to Truth: the Christ was lifted up; and, though he may not know it, some human heart has been drawn nearer the eternal Truth, Christ.

"Then I commenced to work for you, and when the roseate hues of early morning began to steal into the room, the knowledge came to me that there was nothing more to fight--error was overcome. All is well, even the delay which at first seemed altogether wrong. Now I will tell you the reason of it. On Saturday afternoon I was driving your pony in the small basket carriage, which you so often used. (Since they cannot have their little master, both Bob and the pony think the next best thing is to take me about.) I am becoming well acquainted with all the beautiful lanes in the neighborhood, for I frequently take these little excursions.

"We were three or four miles from home, when, in a very narrow lane, where it was impossible to pass another vehicle, we met a farmer, driving a dog-cart. The farmer showed his reluctance to be the one to back out of the lane. He accosted me with these words: 'Ma'am, I am in great haste; it is a matter of life and death.'

"'Indeed,' I said, 'is it the doctor you are in haste to reach?'

"'No,' he replied, briefly, 'the doctor has given her up. It is the lady that lives at Willmar Court I want to see.'

"'Then you have not far to go,' I said. 'She is here. What is your trouble?' Then he told me that his only child, a girl of seven, was believed to be dying. The doctor gave no hope of saving her. 'It seems the news of your beautiful healing has spread through the neighboring villages, and the grief-stricken parents of this little girl thought there might be hope for her.'

"I told the farmer I would go with him, and straightway sent Bob home with the pony, bidding him to tell the servants I should return as soon as possible, but not to trouble if I did not return that night.

"As soon as we had backed out of the lane, the farmer drove furiously, and it was not long before we reached his homestead. I found the belief of death so strong surrounding the child, that it seemed necessary to remain there.

"In two days it was overcome, but I stayed another day to give the wearied mother a good rest. The farmer drove me home last night, when I found everyone sadly troubled. They had begun to fear I was never going to return, and Bob could not give them any idea as to who had driven away with me. The letters and telegrams from Mandeville naturally added to their anxiety.

"Now, all is well: Good was governing--Love leading all the time. I cannot yet understand how it was the bull tossed you. Were you not able to realize your dominion? or was it the mesmerism of fear that seized you? Mrs. Mandeville mentions in her letter that you stood between your little cousins and the bull. My dear boy, of course you would! I could not imagine your doing otherwise. Doubtless the nurse's fear and the cries of the little girls affected you--the contagion of thought. Had you been quite alone, I feel so sure that you would have been able to realize your God-given dominion.

"Tell me more when you write (I am longing for a letter) of the old man and his little grand-daughter. Work always comes to willing hands and loving hearts, and what work is, or ever can be, so beautiful as work for the Master in His Vineyard. Never think any service little. Merely carrying even a cup of cold water will in no case lose its reward. But the joy of working--*of being allowed to work*--is sufficient. We do not look to the reward.

"With loving thoughts,

Believe me always, dear Carol,

Your affectionate cousin,

ALICIA DESMOND."

Before returning to the school-room, Carol sought his aunt in her morning-room. After reading his letters, he always took them to her, and asked her to read them too. They were not, perhaps, always as intelligible to her as they were to the boy, but they never failed to interest her. She was conscious of a growing desire to know the writer, whom she had never met. Later in the day Carol received another letter, delivered by hand. It was from Mrs. Burton, joyfully telling him the doctor was willing for her to take Eloise into Devonshire to his cousin.

He wrote immediately to Miss Desmond, asking her if she would invite Mrs. Burton and her little daughter to the Court, explaining the reason. He knew the invitation would not be long in coming.

CHAPTER XX.--"LIGHT AT EVENTIDE."

On the following Sunday evening Carol appeared at Mr. Higgs' cottage at the usual time.

It seemed almost impossible to believe there had been a break, and that for three days he had lain, to mortal sense, between life and death. So entirely had the cloud rolled away, it was difficult to realize it had ever darkened the horizon.

"I wasn't expecting you, Master Carol, but I'm right glad to see you. It do seem so wonderful that just this time last Sunday all the village was waiting for news from the Manor, and I was that sad thinking I'd never have you come to see me again. The Rector prayed for you in church. I was there for the first time for well-nigh two years. 'Well, well,' I said to myself, 'if the Lord takes him, His will be done.' But, oh, I prayed as I've never prayed since we lost our first child that He wouldn't."

"You do not understand then yet that death can never be God's will. Didn't Jesus say, 'I am come that they might have life, and that they might have it more abundantly'? If Jesus came to bring us life, does not that show that God never sends death?"

"Well, Master Carol, as you put it, maybe it is so, but I'm an old man, and it's what I was taught as a boy, and the belief's grown up wi' me, and somehow I wouldn't like to give up the thought. It's the only thing that makes the parting bearable--to think God wills it. We put it on the headstone where we laid our little girl. *Thy will be done.* Aye, I've stood and looked at them words many a time, and they sort o' comforted me. She was our first-born."

"There is another verse which says 'to know God is everlasting life.' In everlasting life there can be no death, can there? Just think of this: If the sun were never hidden, and you could keep your eyes steadfastly on the light, you would have no knowledge of darkness--you would not understand it or believe in it. In the same way when we understand that God is ALL, we must lose the thought of and belief in death. There is no death to those that know we live and move and have our being in God-Life. Death could not steal one of God's ideas--His children--and destroy it. What seems to die is not God's child. What you buried in the churchyard was not your little girl, and what they cast into the sea, was not my father. They are still living. It is only that we do not see them. You know Jesus says, 'In my Father's house are many mansions.' They have passed on to another mansion--that is all. My cousin has taught me that the mansions

Jesus spoke of are not afar off in a locality called Heaven. We are to-day--you and I--dwelling in one of God's mansions, and it is a higher or a lower mansion according as we dwell in the consciousness of good. We have to take all the steps up to that special place which Jesus has gone to prepare for us. If we are not ready for it, we shall not be able to enter it, even if we have passed through the door called death. We have to fight and overcome all that separates us from God. Jesus overcame everything. He put sin and disease under his feet, and we have just to follow in his steps, knowing that he prepared the way, and is helping us all the time. Perhaps you did not think when you had rheumatism that it was a shadow between you and God, did you? You thought it was God's will for you."

"That's true, Master Carol. I just bowed down to it, thinking God chose to afflict me for some special purpose."

"I knew it was not so, when I tried to help you. I always saw you perfect, as God made you, and you know the shadow disappeared. When I lay in bed a few days ago, and couldn't move, the bruises seemed so real, and the pain very great, I couldn't think of them as shadows, but my cousin was able to do it for me, and all disappeared. Neither my aunt nor the doctor seemed able to believe it at first, because they do not understand. Won't it be a happy day when everyone understands that Truth destroys disease; and when little children have hip-disease doctors won't hurt them to try to make them better, as they did me?"

"Did they really?"

"Yes, and the operation did not make me better. But we will not talk about it. I ought not to remember anything about it. It was all error. Shall we have the chapter again from St. John which tells us 'In my Father's house are many mansions'?"

"Aye, I mind that chapter well. The words just sink down into my heart, and stir up something there, and I've wanted to understand them better. I've thought a lot about it since the last time you talked to me. I know He is faithful who promised, the 'works that I do shall he do also.' As I said before, I'm an old man, Master Carol, and I've been looking for it all my life. Why, I've asked myself, don't His servants and ministers give us the signs He promised?"

"And now what you have been looking for all these years has come--the light at eventide," Carol said softly, looking beyond the old man with eyes that seemed unconscious of the crimson of the setting sun, as he caught a glimpse of that marvellous light which 'never was, on land or sea'--spiritual understanding.

"You have been healed, and your little grand-daughter, and I, too, in the way the Master commanded."

"Aye, it's true, Master Carol. I feel like saying, 'Lord, now lettest thou thy servant depart in peace, for mine eyes have seen thy salvation.' It is His salvation. Maybe when you have read me that chapter from the Bible, you'll read me some pages of the little book which seems to make things clearer to me, and helps me to understand the Bible better."

"I am sorry, I may not," Carol said regretfully, looking at the little book which lay beside the old man's Bible. "My uncle has taken my copy of the book away because he did not wish me to read it. It would not be honorable to read from another copy. It will be given back to me sometime. I do not know how or when. Auntie asked me not to stay long this evening, so I will read the chapter now."

"My daughter'll be sorry she missed coming in. We didn't expect you to-night, Master Carol. She's very grateful to you; her little girl seems quite well now. There's been no return o' the fits. An' my rheumatiz is quite the talk o' th' village. What's took it away? First one and then another asks. When I tell 'em th' Lord's healed me--well, well, they just look at me, as if they thunk th' rheumatiz has gone to my head and turned my brain. Farmer Stubbins says he's coming in one night to have a talk with me, for he's tried many remedies, but his rheumatiz keeps getting worse."

"Give him the little book to read, or tell him to get one for himself," Carol said. Then he read again the chapter he had once before read. At the end he closed the book without comment.

Brightly wishing the old man good-night, he left the cottage.

CHAPTER XXI.--JOYFUL NEWS FROM ELOISE.

Miss Desmond gladly acceded to Carol's desire, and wrote to Mrs. Burton at once to bring her little girl to stay with her.

They left for Devonshire the following week. A month passed before Carol received the promised letter from Eloise. During the time Miss Desmond wrote to him as usual, but beyond mentioning the pleasure it was to her to have his friends staying with her, and what a dear interesting little girl she found Eloise, she did not give any details of their visit. At the end of the month the postman brought one morning a delightfully "fat envelope" addressed to Carol in a round, childish hand. He knew at once it was the long promised letter from Eloise. There was also a shorter one enclosed from Mrs. Burton.

Carol read Eloise's letter first.

"WILLMAR COURT,

1.   DEVON.

"*My dear Carol,*

"I did not forget I had promised to write soon to you. Miss Desmond seemed to wish me not to write just at first. She said you would understand. I think she wanted everyone at Mandeville to forget for a little while all about me. She called it taking their thought off me.

"Now I have so much to tell you. I do not know how I shall get it all in one letter. Dear Carol, I am just the very, very happiest little girl in all the world. I *can walk*. More than that, I can *run*. Isn't it lovely--wonderful! One night I dreamed that I was walking, and when I awoke in the morning the dream seemed so real, I felt it must be true. So I just got out of bed, and I *could walk*. I walked to Mother's bedside. She was so glad and happy. When we saw dear Miss Desmond at breakfast time, and I wanted to thank her, and tell her how much I loved her, she took me to her room, and pointed to a portrait on the wall. Such a sweet, loving face, with white, wavy hair. 'That, dear Eloise,' she said, 'is the portrait of the one you must love. I could not have taken you to the Fountain of Truth to be healed, had she not first shown me the way.' And oh, Carol, I do love dear Mrs. Eddy. How I wish I could tell her so!

"Just for a few days, my legs were so shaky, and I had to keep sitting down. I only walked about a room. Then I was able to go downstairs. At the end of a week Miss Desmond and Mother took me the walk you first took, and

I sat down to rest just where you rested on the stump of the old tree. We waited quite a long time, hoping Birdie would come. And he did, but he stayed only a minute, chirping--'So glad--so glad.' (It was just like that.) Then he flew away as if he were in a great hurry, and that was all he had time to tell us.

"Miss Desmond said: 'Birdie is always busy about his Father's business.' Mother looked puzzled, and I too. We could not understand. Then Miss Desmond said to me, 'God is Birdie's Father too, dear Eloise. Birdie is a spiritual idea; he has no life apart from God. He has his appointed work to do in God's Kingdom. All God's ideas reflect Him--reflect Life, Truth, Love, Goodness. Perhaps Birdie's work is just to voice a note of joy, of harmony.'

"That made me think, Carol, if even a little bird has his appointed task, I, too, must have mine--some work to do for God. I am waiting for it to be made plain to me. Now I have the desire to do it, Miss Desmond says, the work is sure to come. Even if it is only a very little thing at first, I shall be glad to do it.

"Dear Carol, we are so enjoying staying here, Mother and I. I am so fond of all your pets, and feed them every day, and talk to them about you. Before I could walk, Bob used to take me round the grounds in your pony-carriage, and he always talked so much of you, and the time when he used to take you about. He will be so glad when you come home again. All the servants like to hear about you. They love you so much. I have had to tell them ever so many times about the bull, and how you stood and faced him, and did not run away. They are so proud of you. 'The young Master' they call you. I tell Mother, Willmar Court is like a little kingdom, and you the exiled prince.

"Father is coming next week to take us home. Until he sees me walking, I think he cannot quite believe it. He says he wants to have a long talk with Miss Desmond.

"With many loving thoughts, dear Carol, I am,

Your affectionate little friend

ELOISE BURTON.

"P.S. Mother has helped me just a little with this letter, and now she is writing to you herself."

———

Carol could not wait to read Mrs. Burton's letter before giving the joyful news to Mrs. Mandeville. With both letters in his hand, he ran to seek his aunt in her morning-room.

"Auntie, Auntie!" he cried excitedly--"such news! Eloise can walk--more than that, she can run. Isn't it beautiful?"

"Really, Carol? Is it really true?"

"Yes, Auntie, *really*. Will you read Eloise's letter? And oh, may I tell my cousins?"

"Tell them that Eloise can walk? Why, certainly, dear."

"But more than that, Auntie; they will ask what has made her walk, when every one believed she could never walk again. Mayn't I tell them, Auntie, Christian Science has done what the doctors couldn't do?"

"I will think, dear, what you may tell them. Let me see Eloise's letter. Whilst Mrs. Mandeville read the little girl's letter, Carol opened and read Mrs. Burton's.

"WILLMAR COURT,

1.   DEVON.

"*My dear Carol,*

"Eloise herself has written the glad news to you that the use of her legs is perfectly restored. My joyful gratitude is more than can be expressed in words. Yet it even seems that the blessing of this wonderful physical healing is small in comparison with the knowledge we have gained of the Truth, which Jesus said should make us free. Here, amidst the lovely surroundings of your beautiful home, I have lost my old concept of God, and gained instead an understanding of Him, as ever-present Love: infinite Life, Truth, Love.

"It seemed so soon after I was able to see and realize this that my little girl was healed. And oh, Carol, the kindness and gentleness with which dear Miss Desmond has led us up to this understanding, never letting us for a moment cling to her, pointing always away from personality to divine Principle. We must be and are very grateful for her faithful instruction and example, for her life, so consecrated to God that the promised signs are given: 'They shall lay hands on the sick, and they shall recover.' I did not at the time understand your own marvellous recovery from the effects of the encounter with the bull. I do now, and I feel, dear boy, we owe you intense gratitude. It was your steadfast faith in the Christ, Truth, which led me to seek spiritual healing for my little Eloise. The words come to me: 'I, if I be lifted up, will draw all men unto me.' For me the Christ was lifted up, and I was drawn unto Him. May my life henceforth so testify that others may in the same manner be drawn unto Him.

"Please convey my very kind regards to Mrs. Mandeville. She will, I know, rejoice with us.

"Believe me always, dear Carol,

Yours lovingly,

1.

1.　　　　　BURTON."

"It is indeed wonderful and beautiful, Carol," Mrs. Mandeville said as she returned the little girl's letter. I sincerely rejoice with Dr. and Mrs. Burton. I know what a sad trial Eloise's paralysis has been to them."

Then Mrs. Mandeville became aware that Carol was looking up with anxiously expectant eyes, awaiting an answer to a question.

"Dear boy," she said, "if you told your cousins that Christian Science has made Eloise to walk, they would not understand what you meant. Indeed, I do not quite understand, myself--yet. I will come to the school-room with you, and perhaps we can explain to them that Eloise has been healed by faith in the power of God."

With that Carol had to be satisfied, though he longed to explain that it was not faith alone, but faith with understanding: the understanding of God as All-in-all, Omnipotent, Omnipresent Love.

CHAPTER XXII.--THE RETURN OF ELOISE.

When, the following week, Dr. Burton brought his wife and daughter home, both he and Mrs. Burton gratefully spoke of the Science which had healed her. The little girl, in her wheel-chair, had been so familiar an object of compassion to the villagers that, when they saw her walking, they wanted to know what had brought it about. Then Mr. Higgs triumphantly held up a little book.

"It's all in here, bless the Lord," he said. "What's become o' my rheumatiz, you ask. I don't know what's become o' it. I only know it's gone. What becomes o' the darkness when you let the sunshine in? I'm getting to understand it better every day. There's no need to trouble what's become o' error when you let the Truth in."

Then he told them of his little grand-daughter, and how she, too, had lost something. There was no need to say what. All the village had known of the little girl's sad affliction. Many listened to him, and looked curiously at the little book, but only a few believed. It was easier to attribute the healing to nature, or natural causes, than to spiritual laws. The return of Eloise was a great joy to Carol. She was able to tell him much that he wanted to know. He so seldom spoke of his home, Mrs. Mandeville would have been surprised to know how often he had to fight against a sick longing for the dear scenes of his childhood, and the cousin-friend who was now the representative of both father and mother.

The Burtons arrived home too late for Carol to meet them at the station, as he intended.

The next morning he was an early visitor at their house. Eloise had only just finished breakfast.

"Oh, Carol!"

"Oh, Eloise!"

In a moment the two children were locked in each other's arms. Between them was a bond of sympathy which neither could have defined, stronger, more tender, than the tie of human relationship. Then, joyfully, Eloise began to tell him all about her visit. She had so many messages to deliver, and Carol had so many questions to ask, it was lunch time before they were half through. Dr. Burton came in from his rounds. He told them that he had called at the Manor, and had gained Mrs. Mandeville's permission to keep Carol for the rest of the day.

"Thank you so much, Dr. Burton, I am very pleased to stay," Carol said in answer.

Dr. Burton laid both hands on the boy's shoulders.

"My boy," he said gravely, "the pleasure is ours. We owe you a debt of gratitude we can never hope to repay."

The words brought a flush of pleasure to Carol's face. He could not think that he had done anything to deserve such gratitude.

After lunch, when she found the trunks had been unpacked, Eloise showed Carol a little book, Miss Desmond's parting gift to her. It was exactly like the book that had been given to Carol. He took it from Eloise, as she held it out to him, but immediately laid it down on the table. "Shall we do part of the Lesson together, Carol? It will be so nice. I have done part of it every morning with Miss Desmond."

"Yes, I used to," Carol said, and Eloise detected a note of sadness in his voice.

"Do you study it alone now, Carol?" she said.

"No, I never study it at all, Eloise. I have not a book. The book Cousin Alicia gave me Uncle Raymond has."

"Then we can do it together every week from my book, cannot we?"

"No, Eloise, Uncle Raymond took my book away because he did not wish me to study it. Until he gives me permission, I cannot read it with you."

"I am so sorry, Carol. The Rector always speaks so kindly to me when he sees me, I should not mind asking him to let you have it again--shall I? Perhaps he does not know how much you want it."

"Auntie asked him when I was ill, and he would not. I do not think it would be any use for you to ask him, dear Eloise."

"And wouldn't you like to have my book sometimes, Carol?"

"Not without Uncle Raymond's permission. He is my guardian. I must be obedient to his wishes. Don't look sorry, Eloise. It is all right. We can only take one step at a time. It is sure to be given back to me when I am ready to take another step."

"Will my book be taken away from me? Father and Mother are both pleased for me to have it."

"Why, no, Eloise. The lesson I need to learn is perhaps not the lesson you need. Everyone who comes into Science has something to overcome--some particular lesson to master, Cousin Alicia said. Mine is obedience, cheerful,

- 79 -

willing obedience, and every victory of Truth over error makes us stronger."

Then with the *gaieté de coeur* of childhood, the subject was dismissed. Eloise quickly proposed going to the garden where they spent the afternoon, Carol teaching her to play croquet. Peals of merry laughter reached Mrs. Burton as she sat at an open French window, causing her heart anew to overflow with loving gratitude to the One who had "sent His word," and her child was made whole.

When Mrs. Mandeville paid her usual visit to Carol's room that night, she found him with wide-open eyes, a flush of excitement on his cheeks. "I have had such a happy day, Auntie," he said. "I do love Eloise so much, and she loves me, too" (Mrs. Mandeville smiled), "and we both love Cousin Alicia. Since I came to bed I have been trying to think what love is, and it seems it is like light, it can never be described in words. The blind boy in the poem asked,

'What is that thing called light,

Which I can ne'er enjoy?'

No one could tell him to make him understand, could they? So no one could make anyone understand in words what love is. Just as light comes from the sun, and we can only see it with our eyes, so love comes from God, who is Love, and we can only be conscious of it in our hearts. Isn't it St. John, Auntie, who says we have passed from death unto life when we love the brethren? Then just as eyes which cannot see the light are called blind, mustn't it be that hearts which do not love are dead?"

"It seems to follow naturally your line of reasoning, Carol, though I cannot say the thought ever occurred to me before. There is one marked trait in all little children, they are so full of love."

"Yes, Auntie, especially darling Rosebud. She loves everyone. Do you remember when I was ill, and you lifted her on the bed, how she said: 'I do 'ove 'ou so welly much, Tarol'?"

"Yes, dear, I remember. Rosebud often makes me think of a line of one of the poets:

'For a smile of God, thou art.'"

"That is just beautiful, Auntie, and it explains why little children know what love is, before they know anything else, before they even walk or talk."

"Yes, Carol, all great poets seem able to grasp some momentous truth, and give it to the world in a beautiful line or verse."

"Cousin Alicia has given Eloise a copy of *Science and Health* just like the one she gave me, Auntie. Eloise showed it to me, and offered to lend it to me. But it would not be right for me to read it until Uncle Raymond gives me permission, would it? Do you think he may when he knows of Eloise's healing?"

"He does know, dear. I was talking to him last night about it. He attributes it to the change into Devonshire, or--or some other reason. I think he suggested hypnotism."

"But they took her to Germany some time ago, and that change made no difference, nor the great German doctor she was under."

"That is so, dear, still Uncle Raymond will not listen. I think it will be unwise to talk any more on the subject to him."

"Do you think then, Auntie, he will not be willing for me to have the book again until--until I am a man?"

"I fear that may be so, dear."

"Oh, Auntie!"

For a moment the grave eyes filled with tears. The next instant they were dashed away. "What am I thinking of? Error, error, begone! Love *can* find a way, and Love *will* find a way. It is quite all right, Auntie," clasping both arms around her neck.

"Just wait and see! If we are not standing 'porter at the door of thought' every moment, what a lot of wrong thoughts come trooping in."

CHAPTER XXIII.--A LONG-DELAYED LETTER.

That was an eventful week to Carol. Three or four days after the return of Mrs. Burton and Eloise it was his turn to open the post-bag. The daily task of receiving the post-bag, unlocking it, sorting, and then distributing the contents, was always such a pleasure to the elder children that they had agreed to take it by turns.

There seemed an unusually full bag that morning when he emptied the contents on the hall table. He collected into a little pile all the letters for the servants' hall, for the school-room, and for Mrs. Mandeville. Colonel Mandeville was away with his regiment. Quite at the last he discovered two envelopes bearing the small, neat handwriting which always called forth an exclamation of pleasure.

"Two letters this morning from Cousin Alicia, one for Auntie and one for me!"

But he faithfully finished his task, and delivered the letters to their respective owners before opening his own letter.

Mrs. Mandeville frequently breakfasted with the children when Colonel Mandeville was away and there were no visitors staying in the house. Carol found her in the schoolroom.

Breakfast had commenced. "You have had a big delivery this morning, Mr. Postman, have you not?" she said.

"Yes, Auntie, nearly everyone has had more than one letter, and here are four for you, three for Miss Markham, one for Percy, one for Edith, and one for me from Cousin Alicia. One of your letters, too, Auntie, is from Cousin Alicia, and it is quite a fat one. Mine is quite thin. May I open it, Auntie?"

"Certainly, dear, I am sure Miss Markham will allow you. We all know how little people are impatient to read their letters."

Mrs. Mandeville laid three of her letters beside her plate. The one bearing the Devonshire post-mark she held in her hand, and presently drew the contents from the envelope.

Her face grew very white, her hand trembled as she saw Miss Desmond's letter enclosed another. Her eyes, suffused with tears, fell on dear, familiar writing.

Was it a message from the grave--from that watery grave where the mortal remains of the brother still so dear to her had been cast?

Carol meanwhile was devouring his letter, oblivious of everything else. He read:

"WILLMAR COURT,

1.   DEVON.

"*My dear Carol,*

"Something so wonderful and beautiful has happened. Yet I should not perhaps use the word 'wonderful,' since nothing can be lost when Mind governs and controls. The letter which your dear father wrote me just before his death has at last reached me.

"Evidently through a mistake at the sorting office it was slipped into the American mail-bag at Gibraltar instead of the English. My name and address are almost stamped out, it has been to so many places in the United States of America and was afterwards sent on to Canada, where it has also visited many post-offices, before some postmaster or post-mistress remembered that S. Devon is part of an English county.

"A letter so important for your future, dear, could not be lost. I am sending it for Mrs. Mandeville to read, as it is necessary for her and also your Uncle Raymond to know the contents. They will, I am sure, observe their brother's last wishes; and one is, that no hindrance or impediment shall be put in the way of your studying the Science which has healed you. I am to buy a new copy of *Science and Health*, and write in it: 'To Carol--from Father.' You see, dear, Love has found a way, and just the most beautiful way of restoring to you the book you seemed to have lost, for a time at least.

"Dearly as you have valued the book before, it will have an added value with the knowledge that it comes to you expressly by your dear father's desire. Mrs. Mandeville will, no doubt, let you read (or read to you) the letter before returning it to me. You will rejoice to learn how much you were in your father's thoughts at the last. I have ordered a copy of the book. You will receive it in a very short time. I know how glad you will be to be able to study the Lesson-Sermons again. How nice it will be for you and Eloise to do them sometimes together! Dear little girl! Give her many loving thoughts from me. We miss her very much. Bob's affections seem about equally divided between his young master and 'the little lady' as he calls her.

"Always in thought and deed, dear Carol,

Your loving cousin,

ALICIA DESMOND."

Very quietly Carol went to the back of his aunt's chair, and slipping an arm around her neck whispered softly in her ear:

"It's all right, Auntie. I knew that Love would find a way, but I didn't think it would be quite so soon, and such a beautiful way. It is all in Father's letter."

Mrs. Mandeville had laid her letters down unread. She could not disappoint the children, who loved her to breakfast with them, by taking them to her own room, and she wanted to be alone when she read them. As soon as breakfast was over, she left the school-room. An hour later Carol received a message that she wanted him to go to her.

"You have been crying, Auntie," he said, as he entered the room.

"Yes, dear, this letter from your father, and my dear brother, has been a joy and a sorrow to me, bringing back so vividly the remembrance of him. You will like to read it."

She gave the letter to Carol, and he at once sat down beside her, and read it.

"*My dear Alicia,*

"The fiat has gone forth! They give me neither weeks nor days: a few hours only. The sea has been very rough the past three days. A partly healed wound has reopened: the hemorrhage is internal. They cannot stop it. I think of you and my boy, and that Science which stanched his running wounds, and I wish I knew something of it. I put it off, like one of old, to a more convenient season. The little book you gave me I left with some poor fellows in the hospital, intending to get another copy when I reached England.

"Much of what you told me comes back, but it is not enough. I cannot realize it sufficiently. I have absolute faith that if I could reach England, or even cable to you, the verdict would be reversed. Ah, well! a greater man than I is supposed to have said:

'A day less or more, at sea or ashore,

We die, does it matter when?'

Somehow, it does seem to matter now. Life--even this life--has possibilities which I have failed to grasp. With you to help me, it seems I should have gained a clearer understanding of eternal verities. A haze--a mist is creeping over my senses. What I have to write I must write quickly.

"I think you know by a deed of settlement, executed before I left for South Africa, in the event of my death, my brother Raymond, and my dear sister Emmeline, become Carol's guardians. There is no time now to alter that arrangement in any way, even if I wished. It will be good for the boy to be with his cousins. He has seen too little of other children, and Emmeline, I know, will be a mother to him. Both she and Raymond will respect my last wishes, I am sure. Therefore, I want them to know it is my desire for Carol to spend three months of every year with you at his own home, that you may instruct him in that knowledge of God which has healed him. It is recorded that once ten were cleansed, and nine went thankless away. He must not belong to the nine.

"I have explained to Colonel Mandeville my earnest desire that you may be able to live at the Court, keeping on all the old servants until Carol is of age. The last time I saw my brother Raymond, the subject of Christian Science was mentioned, and from the remarks he made, his bitterly antagonistic views of it, I greatly fear that under his guardianship Carol may not be allowed to continue the study. Will you purchase for me a copy of the text-book, *Science and Health*, and write in it:

No one will take from the boy his dying father's last gift, and my wishes regarding it will I know, be paramount with him. He will like to know that my one regret now is that I did not myself study it when I had the opportunity.

"I have faced death before. I am facing it again, as a soldier, and, I trust, as a Christian. Somewhere it is written 'Greater love hath no man'-- You know the rest. Perhaps it will count, though it may not have been love so much as duty prompted the action which is costing me my life.

"I would write to Carol, and to Emmeline. I cannot. The pen slips from my hand."

————

The concluding sentence and the signature were almost illegible. Mrs. Mandeville took Carol in her arms, and they wept together.

"It is so cruel to think he might have been spared to us," she sobbed.

"Yes, Auntie; he would have been," Carol replied with simple faith.

CHAPTER XXIV.--A JOYFUL SURPRISE.

In less than a week a small parcel arrived by post addressed to Carol. He knew before he opened it that it contained the little book which he had so longed for, and which would be, if possible, even dearer to him, henceforth, from the circumstances under which he regained it. He took the little parcel to Mrs. Mandeville's room after breakfast, and opened it there. As he drew the small volume from its cardboard case, he held it up to show her. Then, opening it, he exclaimed in a tone of great surprise, mingled with joy:

"Auntie, it is in dear Father's own handwriting!

'To Carol: from Father.'"

"How can it be?"

Then, as they examined the writing, they saw that Miss Desmond had cut the words from her letter. So neatly had the foreign paper been gummed in, it was not at first noticeable.

"Was it not lovely of Cousin Alicia to think of it, Auntie?"

"It was, indeed, dear. You will always realize now that it is your father's gift."

"Yes, Auntie; my earthly father's and my heavenly Father's, too. I was thinking this morning of that lovely verse in Isaiah: 'Before they call I will answer: and while they are yet speaking I will hear.' And I knew that Love had answered before I called. Before I knew my need, it was met. I am glad the letter was delayed so long, because I have learned so much. 'Every trial of our faith in God makes us stronger,' Mrs. Eddy says. It did seem at first as if I should have to wait years for the book, didn't it? I am glad I was so sure that Love could and would find a way."

As the boy spoke, the Rector walked into the room. In a momentary impulse Carol seized the little book which lay on the table, and held it tightly. A crimson flush suffused his face. The next instant he looked up at his uncle with fearless eyes, and held out the book to him, saying, "Uncle Raymond, Cousin Alicia has sent me the little book Father asked her to get for me, and see--isn't it beautiful?--'To Carol: from Father,' is in Father's own handwriting."

The Rector took the book, examined the inscription, but made no remark.

"Father did not want me to belong to the nine. You would not like me to either, would you, Uncle Raymond?"

"To the nine, boy?--What do you mean?"

"You remember, Uncle Raymond, when Jesus once healed ten lepers, nine went thankless away. I have been healed, and I must acknowledge it at all times, else I should be as one of them."

A frown gathered on the Rector's face.

"Never speak to me, Carol, of your healing in the same breath with the healings of Jesus."

The boy looked sorely pained. For an instant he was silent. In that instant he asked:

"Father-Mother God, lead me."

Then he said:

"May I ask you a question, Uncle Raymond?"

"Certainly, Carol; if it is something you want to know."

"It is something I often think about, Uncle. Are there any 'shepherds in Israel' now? Can you tell me?"

"Why, of course, Carol; Israel typifies the Christian world, and God's ministers are His shepherds."

"Yes, Uncle, that was what I thought. Is God not angry now with the shepherds? I often read the 34th chapter of Ezekiel. God was very angry with the shepherds of that time. He said, 'Woe be to the shepherds, because they had not healed that which was sick, nor strengthened that which was diseased, nor bound up that which was broken, neither had they sought out that which was lost.'"

"There have been times in history, Carol, when God's ministers--His shepherds--have been able to heal the sick, but for generations the healing power has been withheld."

"Yes, Uncle, I understand that. For many centuries before Jesus came the healing power had been lost. He brought it back, and taught his disciples how to heal the sick. Then at the end of only three centuries it was lost; and again after many centuries God has sent a messenger to bring it back, but not everyone will listen to the message."

The boy spoke reflectively, as one thinking aloud, not addressing either his uncle or his aunt.

"Raymond," said Mrs. Mandeville quickly (she noted the growing anger on the Rector's face), "Carol has a way of thinking about things he reads in the Bible. His thoughts have often helped me. He does not mean to--to reproach you. Will you tell me, dear Raymond, have you ever read this book which you condemn so strongly?"

"I have not read it, Emmeline. One does not need to read Mrs. Eddy's books to condemn them. The press criticisms and extracts I have read were quite enough for me. Since Carol's father wished him to have a copy of the book, I cannot keep it from him. Otherwise I should, most certainly. I can only pray that he may ultimately see the error of its teaching."

"The fruit is so good," Mrs. Mandeville said softly. "I can only judge by that, until I have studied the book myself, which I intend to do. I think, Carol, darling, you must run back to the school-room now, or you will be late for lessons. Leave your little book with me. You know it will be quite safe, and come to me after school."

After the boy had left the room Mrs. Mandeville turned to the Rector.

"Now I want to ask you a question, if I may, Raymond, may I?"

"Why, of course, Emmeline, you know perfectly well I shall be happy to answer any question you wish to put to me--if I can."

"It is this, Raymond: the Apostle bids us, 'Let this mind be in you which was also in Christ Jesus.' How would you define the 'Mind' simply, that I may grasp it?"

The Rector's memory went back to a Sunday morning some months before when he had preached what he considered a very eloquent sermon from that verse in Philippians. Had his sister forgotten it?

"Do you forget, Emmeline, that I preached from that text not so very long ago? I took as the keynote of my sermon, humility--the humility of Jesus. From the context that was undoubtedly what Saint Paul meant."

"Yes, Raymond, I remember the sermon perfectly; but I cannot feel that to possess humility, even in a superlative degree, would be to possess, as the Apostle commands, the 'Mind' of Christ. Carol was thinking out this subject, in the way he has of thinking about verses in the Bible, and the thought he gave me seems nearer to it. He could see only love. The mind that was in Christ was love. Now, Raymond, if we, at this moment, possessed hearts full of love we could not criticise or condemn anyone or any sect. We could not hold up creeds or dogmas, and say, 'It is necessary to believe this or that because it is a canon of the Church.' We should just know that we and they had passed from death unto life when we love the brethren, and all are brethren who look to the Lord Jesus Christ as an elder brother."

"It seems to me, Emmeline, that even before reading the book you have imbibed some of its mischievous statements. Remember, it teaches a religion of negation. According to Christian Science we have no Heavenly Father, no personal God; nothing but a divine Principle, an eternal existence, to worship."

"Oh, Raymond, you do make a mistake. How can you infer that if you have not studied the book?"

"My authority, Emmeline, for the statement, is Dr. Hanson. He wrote a pamphlet on Christian Science, issued by the Religious Tract Society."

"It seems strange, Raymond, that a man of Dr. Hanson's eminence should write, and the Religious Tract Society should publish, a statement so misleading,--a statement which a boy of Carol's years could easily confute. Carol prays to, and speaks of his Heavenly Father in a way which, I grieve to say, my own children never do. Only a few minutes before you entered the room, he said that this little book was a gift not only from his earthly father but from his Heavenly Father, too. So how can there be no Heavenly Father to a Christian Scientist? It is true he speaks more frequently of Him as Divine Love; and it seems to me he has a more comprehensive idea of God than I have myself, for the thought has often presented itself to me, how can we, as the Scriptures say, 'live, move and have our being' in Him, if God is a person, according to our idea of personality? The idea which Carol has given me of God as infinite Love, filling the universe like light, makes that verse more intelligible."

"A discussion such as this, Emmeline, cannot be productive of any good. I will send you that little pamphlet I mentioned."

"Thank you, Raymond. I will read it after I have read *Science and Health*."

The Rector then changed the conversation, and spoke of the object of his visit to the Manor that morning.

CHAPTER XXV.--A LITTLE SERVICE.

On the following Sunday evening Carol started at the usual time for Mr. Higgs' cottage, carrying with him the little, much-valued book and with it the current *Quarterly* which Miss Desmond had also sent him. His surprise was great, on arriving at the cottage, to find Mrs. Burton and Eloise there. They knew the prohibition was removed, and Carol was free to read and study *Science and Health*.

"We thought you would come, Carol," Eloise exclaimed. "We wanted to hear you read the Lesson-Sermon. It will be quite a little service, won't it?"

"Yes, dear Carol; we thought we should like to join you this evening," Mrs. Burton said. "We are only the 'two or three gathered together,' but we are all of one mind. So it will be a little service, as Eloise says."

Presently Mr. Higgs' daughter and his little grand-daughter came in.

It was arranged for Mrs. Burton to read the Bible verses, and for Carol to read the quotations from *Science and Health*. At the close of the Lesson-Sermon Carol and Eloise sang together, from the Christian Science Hymnal, the hymn which both knew and loved,--

"Shepherd, show me how to go."

The beauty of the words, and the young voices blending in perfect harmony, brought tears of emotion to the old man's eyes.

"Aye, ma'am," he said to Mrs. Burton afterwards, "who but the Shepherd himself, is leading us into those green pastures where the fetters that bound us are loosed? There's a many things I can't pretend to understand, and the old beliefs grip hard, but I just hold on, and know it must be the Truth which the Master promised should make us free. It's the tree that is known by its fruits. I'm sorry Rector's so set up against it. But there, it was the priests and scribes who persecuted the Master himself. Seems to me it would not be the Truth if the world received it gladly."

"I believe you are right in thinking that, Mr. Higgs. In whatever period of the world's history Truth has been recognized, and demonstrated, its adherents were always persecuted and stoned. Jesus reminded his persecutors that they stoned the prophets which were before him."

"Yes, ma'am, I know it is the glorious Truth which has loosed my rheumatiz, and made me free, and I am just ashamed to confess to you and Master Carol that just lately thoughts I can't get rid of come tormenting me. In this way: I go sometimes to church, but I feel no pleasure in the service.

It has lost its hold o' me. Then I think o' Father and Mother, o' blessed memory. They lived and died with no thought o' beyond what the Rector could give them. It sort o' troubles me to think I am going away from what they trusted to. The Rector then was an old man. Why, ma'am, if ever a saint o' God walked this earth, he was one. If he passed down the village street, you'd see all the children run to him, clustering round him. When he looked at you, it didn't seem to need any words: it was just as if he said, 'God bless you.' His smile was a blessing. So I just ask myself, Why wasn't the sick healed when he prayed for them, if it was right and God's will for them to be healed? Surely, he was a servant of God."

"I propounded a similar question, Mr. Higgs, to the lady I have been staying with in Devonshire, Carol's cousin, Miss Desmond. It has been my great privilege to know many saintly characters, whose lives testified to their faith. My own mother was such a one. Yet, for many years, she was a great sufferer. I asked Miss Desmond why such loving faith in God and Jesus the Christ, had not always brought physical healing. What we call the orthodox church, also Non-conformity, has nurtured souls for heaven. We cannot, therefore, condemn its teaching. Miss Desmond said it is not for us to judge or to criticise either individuals or other churches. We all, individually and collectively, can only grasp the truth as far as we apprehend it, and we must not harbor a troubled thought that in becoming Christian Scientists we are leaving any church to which we once belonged. We are simply moving forward--stepping upward to a higher platform. It is the law of progression. A child at school does not regret being moved to a higher class. Neither have we anything to regret, even if we entirely sever our connection with the church of our childhood. Even now, for the most advanced Christian Scientists there is yet a higher platform to be reached, since Mrs. Eddy says, in *Science and Health*, 'All of Truth is not understood.' All we have to do at the present is to live up to--to demonstrate, the highest that we know. You in your walk of life, I in mine; and these dear children, who, spiritually, have touched the hem of Christ's garment and have been healed, in theirs."

"Thank you, ma'am, I'll try to think of it, as you've kindly explained it. There's another old belief I can't see clearly to get rid o' yet, though Master Carol tried to make me see it's wrong, and that is 'Thy will be done,' on the tombstones in the churchyard. I can see that sin and disease can never be God's will; but death may sometimes be a sort o' messenger from God to call us home."

Mrs. Burton smiled.

"Yes; many poets have eulogized death as a 'bright messenger.' But in the light of Christian Science we know it cannot be: evil can never under *any* circumstance change into good--an enemy--the last enemy--into a friend. Think for one moment how Jesus taught us to pray 'Thy will be done on earth *as it is in heaven.*' Then ask yourself: Is death God's will in heaven? If not, then it cannot be on earth. I quite see now why many petitions have failed to bring an answer. The pleading lips have besought God to reverse 'His decree,' the decree that never was His. We learned that, Eloise, darling, did we not, in Devonshire?"

"Yes, Mother; and when we quite understood why my lameness was never God's will for me, I lost it."

"So the world, Mr. Higgs, must change its old belief, and realize that death is an enemy which inevitably will one day be destroyed. In God's spiritual Kingdom, sin, disease, and death find no place. Now I think we must all bid you good-night, or it will be dark before Carol reaches the Manor. The evenings draw in so quickly, now. We will walk part of the way with you, Carol," Mrs. Burton said as they left the cottage. They had not gone very far when they met Mrs. Mandeville.

"Auntie," Carol exclaimed joyfully, "were you coming to meet me?"

"Yes, dear. I found you had not returned. As I did not quite like your coming alone through the park, I came to meet you."

After a little conversation with Mrs. Burton and Eloise, Mrs. Mandeville and Carol walked home together, Carol clinging affectionately to his aunt's arm.

"It is nice to have you to walk home with me, Auntie; but I wish you would never have a thought of fear for me."

"I'll try not to another time, darling. As I walked along I remembered something, Carol. Since that day when you came to my room I have never had one of my old headaches. They used to be so painfully frequent. Did you charm them away?"

"No, Auntie; but I knew you had not learned how to 'stand porter at the door of thought.' So I just stood there for you; and error cannot creep back when the sword of Truth is raised against it."

Mrs. Mandeville's only answer was to stoop and kiss the boy's upturned face. The words, so simple, grave, and sweet, had gone straight to her heart.

CHAPTER XXVI.--CONCLUSION.

The calendar of months named December, and before it, excited, expectant little people stood daily, counting first the weeks, then the days to that one day of all the year which the children love best.

Carol had to listen again and again to all the wonderful and mysterious things which always happened at the Manor on Christmas Eve and Christmas Day. Price lists and illustrated catalogues were the only books in requisition after lessons were over. The elder children wondered how they could have bought their Christmas presents if there were no parcel post. Carol was especially the helper and confederate of the three little girls in the nursery. He assisted them in choosing their "surprises," wrote the letters, and enclosed the postal orders; and certainly, from the marvellous list of things they were able to purchase, their little accumulated heap of pennies must, in some magic way, have changed into sovereigns in his hands. The joyful excitement of the three little girls, when the parcels arrived, gave Carol the greatest pleasure he had ever known. Only Nurse was allowed to be present when the parcels were opened, and she promised to lock them securely away where no one could catch a glimpse until they were brought out on Christmas eve.

It wanted only one week to Christmas day, when Rosebud came to the school-room one morning, saying: "Mover wants 'ou, Tarol."

Carol went at once to his aunt's room. She was sitting with an open letter in her hand, a rather graver than usual expression on her face. "Carol, dear," she said, "for some little time I have been thinking I ought to let you go home for Christmas. It seems to me it is what your dear father would wish; but I could not let you take the long journey alone and there seemed no other way until this morning. I have just received a letter from a dear old friend in which she mentions that she will be travelling to Exeter in two days' time. So I could take you to London to meet her there, and you could travel with her to Exeter, where Miss Desmond might meet you. I do not like to part with you, even for a month or six weeks, my 'little porter at the door of thought.'"

"Auntie, it won't make any difference if I am here, or in Devonshire. I can still bar the door to error."

"Yes, dear; I believe you can. It is really not that only. I am thinking we shall all miss you so. You seem to be everyone's confederate for their Christmas surprises. Would you rather go, or stay, dear?"

"I should be happy to stay here, or happy to go home for Christmas, Auntie."

"Yes; I think you would, dear. So we must consider other people. Miss Desmond, I know, would rejoice to have you, and it seems the right of both tenants and servants to have the 'little master' amongst them at Christmas. So I have decided it will be right to let you go."

But when this decision was made known in the school-room and nursery there were great lamentations. No one had given a thought to the possibility of Carol not being with them for the Christmas festivities; and Mrs. Mandeville was besought again and again not to let Carol go home before Christmas.

But, having well considered the matter, she was firm. A telegram was at once despatched to Miss Desmond apprising her of the arrangement. The answer that quickly came satisfied Mrs. Mandeville that she had been led to make a right decision. Brief but expressive was Miss Desmond's wire: "Great rejoicings on receipt of news. Will gladly meet Carol at Exeter."

There was yet another little person to whom the news was not joyful. Eloise's lips quivered and her blue eyes filled with tears when she heard. Carol was so much to her, and she to him. She thought of him as a brother; and a sister of his own name could not have been more tenderly loved by the boy. The bond between them was closer and dearer than that of human relationship.

"It will be only just at first, Eloise, that we shall seem to be far apart. Then you will be able to realize there is no distance in Mind. At first, when I came here, I seemed to be so far away from Cousin Alicia; but I never feel that now. I just know her thought is with me, and thought is the only real. It will be lovely to hear her voice again, and to feel my hand clasped in hers, but still that won't make her very own self nearer to me."

"I do not quite understand--yet, Carol," Eloise answered a little sadly. Then she had some news to give him. Early in the New Year the Burtons were going to live in London. True to his promise, Dr. Burton was giving up his medical practice, and was going to join that little band of men and women whose lives are consecrated to the work of destroying the many manifestations of sin and disease, in the way the Master taught.

"And, when you come back to the Manor, Carol, we shall not be here."

Eloise in one sentence regretfully summed up the situation.

"I shall miss you, dear Eloise. But you will write to me, and I shall write very often to you, and when I go home in the summer, perhaps Mrs.

Burton will let you come, too. Then Cousin Alicia will be happy to have both her children in Science with her."

"That will be lovely, Carol! I am sure Mother will like me to visit Miss Desmond again. It seems a long time to look forward to, but time really passes very quickly. Sometimes the days are not long enough for all I want to do. I am to go to school when we live in London. All the beautiful things I have longed for are coming to me. Carol, I do wish every little girl and every little boy knew how to ask Divine Love for what they want. When I am older that is the work I want to do,--to teach other children as Miss Desmond taught me."

"And I, too, Eloise. Love is so near, but we didn't know it till we learned it in Science, did we?"

"No, Carol; I didn't know it, when I used to sit all day in my little wheelchair, longing to walk like other children. It was like living in a dark room until some one came and opened the shutters to let the sunlight in. The sunlight was there all the time, but I did not know it. I was God's perfect child all the time, but I believed I was lame, until Miss Desmond taught me the Truth."

"When I go to bed, Eloise, thoughts come to me. I tell them to Auntie sometimes, but not to any one else. Shall I tell you what I was thinking last night?"

"Please, Carol, I should like to know."

"I began first by thinking if any one asked me, where is heaven, I should answer: Heaven is where God is. Then I remembered, God is *everywhere*. There is no place where God is not. Then I knew that everywhere must be heaven, and we have only to open our eyes, and just as much as we can see of good--God--just that far we shall have entered heaven. So it won't matter, Eloise, if you are in London, and I am in Devonshire, if we are both looking steadfastly all the time to see only good around us, we shall both be entering the Kingdom of Heaven. There is only one gate--a golden gate-- into that Kingdom, and 'Christ in divine Science shows us the way.'"

The little country station seemed to be quite full of people when the train that was to carry Mrs. Mandeville and Carol to London drew up at the platform. The hour they were to leave had become known in the village, and, besides all his cousins, their nurses and Miss Markham, Mr. Higgs, his daughter and grand-daughter, Dr. and Mrs. Burton, and Eloise were there. At the last moment the Rector hurriedly stalked in.

"Almost too late, dear Raymond," Mrs. Mandeville said as he greeted them.

"So, Carol, I learn you have succeeded in planting Christian Science in this village."

The boy looked up with his quiet, fearless eyes.

"Not I, Uncle Raymond!"

"Who then?"

The boy's head was bowed as he reverently answered: "Christ. I am happy, Uncle Raymond, if I have been a little channel for Truth. I could do nothing myself."

Carol met the grave look on the Rector's face with his bright smile.

"You *are* glad, are you not, Uncle Raymond, that Mr. Higgs and his little grand-daughter, and dear Eloise--I, too--have found the Christ, and have been healed?"

The engine gave a shrill whistle. Mrs. Mandeville drew the boy farther into the carriage; a porter closed the door as the train began to move; the question was unanswered. Mr. Higgs waved his hat, saying fervently, "God bless 'ee, Master Carol; and bring you back to us soon."

Eloise ran along the platform, holding Rosebud by the hand, wafting kisses to be carried to Miss Desmond. When the train was out of sight and she returned to join the others, she saw the Rector was watching her with the kindly smile his face used to wear in the days when she was not able to run about. Clingingly clasping his arm, looking up to him in her winning way, and remembering the question which to Carol had been unanswered, she said: "You *are* glad, are you not, Rector, that I can run about, and that I have been taught the Truth that makes us free?"

"Yes, little girl, I am very glad. Perhaps I have been mistaken in my judgment. Tell me, Eloise, what is this Truth of which you speak?"

Eloise hesitated a moment; then, looking up beyond the Rector into the broad blue heavens, she said: "It is just *knowing* that God is *All*, and there is nothing beside. All the *real* God made; whatever He did not make is shadow. When I quite understood that God could not make an imperfect thing--that He never, never made a lame little girl--the shadow disappeared, and I could walk."

The Rector turned to Mr. Higgs who was standing near. "Is that what my nephew has been teaching you, Higgs?"

"Yes, sir; but I've been slower to grasp it. Seems to me the Truth is very simple, but we need the childlike mind to take it in."

"Maybe you are right, Higgs--maybe you are right. 'Whosoever shall not receive the kingdom of God as a little child ... shall not enter therein.' The Master's words."

Thoughtfully, with bent head and downcast eyes, meditating deeply, the Rector walked back to the Rectory. Words very familiar came to him with a different meaning: "Ye shall know the Truth, and the Truth shall make you free;" and with the words came a desire that was prayer: "Lord, teach me this Truth. Grant me the childlike mind."

————

"Carol, I have been thinking of something," Mrs. Mandeville said, as the train bore them along.

"Should you like to know of what I have been thinking?"

"Please, dear Auntie; I should very much like to know."

"Well, dear, I have been thinking if it should occur to the young Master of Willmar Court to send Rosebud and me an invitation whilst he is at home, we should accept it."

"Oh, Auntie, what a lovely thought! To have you and Rosebud, and Cousin Alicia, all together!"

"I want Miss Desmond, Carol, to teach me some of the things she has taught you."

There was a long silence. The boy's heart was too full for words. Then he said: "Auntie, I know now how the little bird felt when the King opened the cage door, and he sang and sang for joy. My heart is singing to *my* King. I wonder if--perhaps--He will say, some missing note has come into Carol's song."

"Indeed, my darling, I think so."

He nestled closely beside her. Looking down she saw on his face the reflection of a great joy--a great peace; and she knew that he had just crept into Love's arms.

"He that dwelleth in the secret place of the Most High shall abide under the shadow of the Almighty.... He shall cover thee with His feathers, and under His wings shalt thou trust. His Truth shall be thy shield and buckler."

PSALM 91.